Legends Reborn

and other stories

Carol Hightshoe

WolfSinger Publications ⚡ Security, Colorado

Midnight Song – First published in Creature Fantastic – 2001
Snipe Hunt – First published in Galaxy Fest Program Book – 2012
Life in the Shadows – First published in The Fractured Publisher – 2005
The Final Blessing – First published in Stories of Strength – 2005
The Sword of Power – First published in Illuminated Manuscripts – 2005
The Gift of All – First published through Amazon Shorts – 2006
Adrift – First published in Space Pirates – 2008
The Second Horseman – First published in The 5th Di – 2008
The President's Meow – First published in Aofie's Kiss – 2009
Cave of Sorrows – First published in Supernatural Colorado – 2015
The Last Defenders – First published in Six Guns Straight From Hell – 2010
Legends Reborn – First published in Pangaia Magazine – 2004
Time of the Month – First published in Different Dragons – 2014
A Story of Inyudo – First published in Healing Waves – 2011
Mr. Zombie Goes to Washington – First published in Zombiefied – 2011
The Cup of Life – First published in It Lives – 2011
Wolves of the Comanchería – First published in Showdown at Midnight – 2011
A Game of Marbles – First published in Beyond Centauri – 200 6
Eternal Escapes – First published in Time Traveling Coffers – 2012
To Live – First published in All About Eve – 2010
Pawn's Gambit – First published in Jim Baen's Universe – 2007
Midnight Ritual – First published in New Realm Magazine – 2015

ISBN 978-1-942450-19-1

Printed and bound in the United States of America

Table of Contents

Midnight Song

How many times have I come here? I can no longer count the days, months or years. The passage of time has no effect on me. I remember when I would come to greet the rising sun. Dawn reflecting hope in the brightening sky and warming earth. Now, I am banished to the nadir of night; when all is dark, and hope only a dream.

It was a year ago, mayhap two, when the priests came and laid their blessing on this place. This small valley was sanctified and made anathema to me, or rather to what I have become. Despite this, I am still compelled to come. Each night I sit beside this stone marker and sing of my sorrow. The moon and stars listening to the pain in my soul as I tell them about the loss of my beloved Adairia. I take some comfort in the silence of the night. A silence that only listens and does not judge.

My song awakens the priests and they stand at their small windows saying prayers for protection. I shake my head at the sharp, bittersweet smell of their fear and hatred.

Tonight, as I sit here and raise my gaze to the moon, I feel a stirring in the air. Something is happening. Nothing like this has ever occurred before. My spine tingles. The hair along my neck rises. My claws grasp at the dirt. I whine softly. Looking closely, I see a shimmering before me. A shape is forming. It is wispy. Not wholly there. My nose only detects the dustiness of the earth and the biting scent of the trees surrounding this area. The shape begins to solidify. Suddenly, the perfume of heather fills the air. I inhale deeply. Heather was always her favorite flower.

It is her! I have not seen her since that horrific night—so long ago. The night the curse struck and she vanished from my life.

She is much as I remember her: Tall, with dark eyes and dark hair. Her delicate features highlighted by the glow surrounding her as she stands next to the stone bearing her name. Her eyes meet my own and there is a deep sadness reflected in them.

A soft creak comes from the door of the small church. I see one of the priests step outside. Startled I rise and turn to flee. She begins to fade.

"Wait," he calls. "Please stay. I am Father Gregory; I mean you no harm."

I glance up at her and she nods slowly, so I sit back down and look at the approaching priest. He is an old man whose eyes, even in this darkness glow with an inner light. Despite the hesitation in his steps, there is a confidence in his stance. As he approaches, he holds out both hands to show he is carrying nothing. I smell his fear, but it is accompanied by something else. A fragrance both soft and strong, the smell of flowers in a meadow, of rain, of a sunrise; the scent of love, compassion and hope.

Father Gregory glances at her, then at the stone marker with its single word scratched into its surface. "Adairia?" he asks.

She nods. Glancing at me, Adairia smiles that small wistful smile I have not seen in so long.

I nod my understanding of her unspoken request. Closing my eyes, I concentrate on triggering a change I have not experienced since that day.

The change comes slowly, and I whimper as I feel my limbs lengthen and my nose flatten. I find myself stretched out on the ground as my senses return. Slowly, I push myself into a sitting position; every joint in my body feels as if it is on fire. I had forgotten the pain involved.

The night air is chill against my bare skin as I stand, and I shiver. Father Gregory hands me his cloak and I wrap myself in its warmth. I look at my hands and frown. The smoothness of the skin is strange after all these years. Sniffing the air around me, I can no longer discern as many different smells as before, yet the scent of heather lingers in the air.

I see Father Gregory watching me closely, his right hand holding the cross on the chain around his neck. Smiling, I extend my hand to him. "I am Leathan."

He takes my hand in a strong clasp and returns the smile.

Gathering the borrowed cloak around me, I sit on the damp ground. Adairia sits beside me and lays a hand on mine. There is warmth in the contact. Looking at her, I see color in her face. I reach up and caress her cheek, she smiles. We look at each other for several minutes, savoring the feel of flesh on flesh.

"Forgive me, Father, for I have sinned," she says, turning back to the priest. "It has been too many years since my last confession."

"It was this sin which condemned you to remain here?" Father Gregory asks, his voice non-judgmental as he looks from her to me.

"Yes." She sighs softly. "It condemned Leathan, also."

Listening to her talk to Father Gregory, I think back on that day so long ago. The day we were married.

~ * ~

The wedding ceremony and celebration had continued until late. The midnight hour was fast approaching when Adairia and I finally made our way back to the home we were to share. The lantern I carried illuminated the sprays of heather woven around the door.

"Leathan, they're beautiful," she said, taking one of the sprays and holding it close to her face.

"Lady Adairia, if I may?" I held my arms out to her.

"Of course." She wrapped her arms around me and kissed me lightly as I started to gather her in my arms.

A sudden burning coursed down my limbs and began to engulf my whole body. Adairia stepped back and dropped the spray of heather.

"No!" I heard her cry as I fell to the ground.

Just as suddenly as it had started, the pain stopped. The dropped spray of heather lay at my feet, its soft lavender now faded to gray. I tried to stand, but could not. Fur covered my limbs and I realized the truth of what I had become. How did this happen? The curse had already struck my family this generation; it shouldn't have been able to strike again.

I glanced around for Adairia and saw no sign of her. I tried to call her name, but only a howl came from my throat.

Not knowing what to do, I ran. Throughout the night I ran, until I came to this small valley. The scent of the heather reminded me of Adairia as I sat and sang of my sorrow.

With the rising of the sun, I felt the fire consuming my body again as the wolf form I had worn during the night left me. I remained here the rest of the day. I could not return to Adairia, not like this. Harailt had vowed vengeance when she chose me over him. This was the form it had taken.

Moonrise found me still here. I raised my voice to the moon, singing of my loss to the watching stars. My throat sore when my song finally faded away.

After several minutes of watching the heather sway in the breeze, I reached out and rubbed my paw on the large rock, my claws leaving a visible mark. With more effort, the scratches dug deeper in the stone. Very slowly, I used my claws to scratch Adairia's name into the rough surface. When I finished, the letters were firm and strong. The racing, tumbling beat of my heart not evident in the straight, clear lines.

The next morning, I fought the change back to human form, and have remained a wolf ever since. The form most suited to my sorrow and solitude.

~ * ~

"Leathan, I'm sorry," Adairia says, bringing me out of my memories.

"Why? I was the one who left and never came back."

"It was my fault, though," she says.

I look at her and she looks away. Reaching out, I gently grasp her chin and turn her face back towards me. "How can that be?"

Her eyes refuse to meet mine, darting between me and the priest standing quietly. He nods and smiles gently at her.

"I knew what Harailt planned as his vengeance." Her voice breaks as she speaks. "We should have postponed the wedding. Found a way to prevent the curse from striking. Something. Anything, but what you were condemned to."

I shake my head and smile, hoping it is a human smile and not the bared tooth smile of a wolf. "Adairia, we both knew about Harailt's threat," I say. "We made the decision to go ahead with the wedding together."

The curse of the werewolf is an ancient one in my family. Earlier that spring my younger brother had been afflicted. As the curse only claims one victim each generation, my family believed I was safe.

I reach down and take her hands in mine. She looks at me,

her face wet with tears. "It was a long time ago and it is something which belongs in the past," I say. "What I don't understand is why we are both still here."

"I did not want to live without you. In my sorrow, I lost the will to live. A few months after our marriage, I died from an illness I no longer had the strength or desire to fight. My spirit was trapped here, in this valley. We are bound together, Leathan—you and I."

"Leathan," Father Gregory says softly. "There is no way the curse itself can be broken. However, it is possible to release you from this immortality. Once you two are no longer bound together, you will live the remainder of a natural life. You must release Adairia."

My mind races in confusion. I must release Adairia. How can I do that? I hesitate.

Glancing at Adairia, I see her dark eyes watching me closely. Those eyes filled with love and sorrow. Studying her face, I realize how strongly I still love her. Just as her love for me caused her to die from her sorrow, my love for her bound her here after that death.

"Adairia, be free," I whisper. I lift her hands to my lips and kiss them gently. Releasing her hands, I stand and step back slowly.

I watch as Father Gregory raises his cross and says something in a language I do not understand. The moonlight grows stronger and bathes Adairia as she begins to fade from view.

"No!" she cries. "Leathan, I do not want to leave you."

The moonlight fades and the mist swirls, concealing her from my sight. When the fog lifts, a female wolf stands where Adairia was. I glance at her and then at the priest. Once again, I trigger the change. This time there is no pain, and I find myself standing nose to nose with Adairia.

"Go in peace, my children." Father Gregory makes the sign of the cross over us both. "My blessings and God's on you both. May you always find sanctuary and welcome in this place."

Adairia and I bow our heads to the priest, then leave. Our strides matching perfectly as we lope off into the forest together. Always together.

Snipe Hunt

"Hey, Billy Ray did you see the lights in the sky last night?" Jimmy Lee asked.

"Yep. Most likely swamp gas or some such," I said looking up at my younger cousin. As usual the boy was a mess. Most of the time he reminded me of the "pig pen" character from the Charlie Brown Christmas special. If we'd ever had snow here in the bayou I just knew he'd build a gray snowman.

"Ned says he heard noise like an engine. Maybe t'were airplanes," Jimmy Lee said.

I shook my head; the boy still seemed to think the stories about the way the world was before the last war, were the way it was now. Guess the kid needed something to believe in. And there really weren't no harm in hoping things might eventually return to normal. "Naw, been no airplanes around here for a while now," I finally said. Unfortunately, hope was all it was.

"Maybe it was one of them unidentified flying objects?"

"Now Jimmy Lee, you know better than that. UFOs was nothing more than secret government projects designed to keep people talking bout them and not prying into other secret government projects. Since there be no more government; there be no more secret government projects and no more UFOs."

"Well, it weren't no swamp gas. Ned says he heard engine noises and I believe him."

"And Ned's the one who took you snipe hunting as well," I said with a grin. "Guess that makes him all trustworthy and what not now don't it."

Jimmy Lee's face turned red and he turned to walk away. I'll never understand why that boy continued to listen to Ned after that. Granted, taking youngsters on the infamous snipe hunt is a tradition that has been around for longer than any of us can remember. Since the changes that took place since the last war we do have to plan them a bit more carefully.

No one rightly knows what truly caused the changes; some

say it was use of nukes in the atmosphere that shut down all the tech stuff and caused the mutations. Whatever it was, the cities were no place to be anymore, particularly at night. Them so-called civilized folks had become nothing more than feral dogs; scavenging and hunting in packs.

Ned decided to do this particular hunt on a night of the full moon; a night when the wild 'uns are usually out. And he thought it would be funny to plan the hunt near town. I think he was hoping for one of them mutants to wander into the area in order to scare Jimmy Lee. I doubt he was planning on Jimmy Lee having to fight his way through a small horde of them to get back that night.

"Jimmy Lee, you want a chance to get even with Ned?" I held out a burlap sack, just like the ones we used on a snipe hunt.

"Ned ain't stupid enough to fall for a snipe hunt," Jimmy Lee said.

"I reckon not, but he might be fool enough to fall for an *alien* hunt."

That made Jimmy Lee smile and he glanced up at the sky. "Yeah, I think he might just be fool enough for that."

~ * ~

"Looks like the boy may have been right bout them being UFOs," Ned said as he pointed to a nearby tree.

I only nodded as Ned touched a small pool of silver liquid that lay in a small hollow on the branch. Now I understood why Jimmy Lee collected several old thermometers before he left to lay the trail for the hunt. This couldn't be a true snipe hunt in the traditional sense as neither of us would have been able to convince Ned to hold a bag while we chased the "alien" down a ravine for him to capture. So, Jimmy Lee had figured on laying a false trail through the bayou and leading Ned around half the night before we ended up back at my cabin. I was along to make sure Ned didn't shoot Jimmy Lee if he actually caught up to the boy.

"There." Ned raised his shotgun and nodded toward something glowing behind a thick curtain of moss hanging from several large cypress trees.

"Wait." I placed a hand on the gun and pushed it down slightly. "We don't even know what that is."

Something crashed through the trees behind me and I spun

around to see Jimmy Lee running toward us. The boy was as white as if he seen a ghost. The old uniform he had put on as a costume was ripped in several places and one of the pointed ears he had stuck over his own was gone.

"Jimmy Lee?" Ned lowered the gun and stared at the boy. He then turned and looked at me. "You two thought to fool me— didn't ya."

Yeah," Jimmy Lee said between breaths. "But this weren't no part of it. There's a real alien ship over there." He pointed toward the glow.

"Jimmy Lee what did I tell you bout UFOs." I slapped the boy lightly on the back of the head.

"Billy Ray, I'm serious. There's a real alien ship over there and real aliens. They ain't no cute little ET's either. They're mean ones. They've been out hunting mutants."

"Well that's good for us. Maybe we can make friends." Ned glanced toward the glow.

"Only one way to find out," I said.

"You two're both crazy. I dun told ya, this ain't no part of our snipe hunt. Billy Ray listen to me. This is real."

"Come on, Billy Ray. Let's go check out those there aliens," Ned said grinning. He shouldered his shotgun and pushed his way through the hanging moss then stopped.

I found myself staring at what appeared to be a large, silver flying saucer; just like the ones that use to be in the movies. Two large aliens, and they were aliens, were standing next to a long ramp that led up into the saucer. Both stood about seven feet tall, were dark skinned with long black clumps of hair. Their necks were ridged on either side and they had tails. Both were also holding some sort of firearm—short and compact, but still obviously a weapon.

The two aliens glanced toward a group that was coming back to the ship. They had several mutants on some sort of sled. They looked like a hunting party returning with their kills.

"See I told ya," Jimmy Lee said.

"Shush," Ned and I said together.

Another of the aliens walked down the ramp and looked at the bodies. "This is all this planet has to offer?" The voice was harsh and guttural, but the language was English.

"Not very worthy opponents," one of the others said.

"True, even after the first few were killed, the rest just kept coming toward us," another said.

"The Commission was correct then; there is no intelligent life on this planet." That was the first one again; I figured it must be the one in charge of the group.

"The life forms may be unique, but there is nothing to indicate they are worth preserving. The Commission will most likely grant permission to go ahead with full colonization."

"Colonization?" Jimmy Lee whispered.

"That's what it said."

"Hey, how is it we're able to understand them things?" Jimmy Lee asked.

"Maybe they have some sort of translation device. Kinda like all them television shows," I said.

"Like hell any talking gator's gonna colonize my home," Ned said raising his shotgun and taking a step forward. "We got more'n enough of the normal variety."

"Ned!" Jimmy Lee started to grab the shotgun.

"Now, let's not be too hasty here," I said stepping out next to Ned. I hoped the aliens would be surprised long for me to finish talking before they started shooting. "Obviously these folks are interested in hunting rare and worthy opponents. Perhaps we should introduce them to one of the most dangerous and elusive opponents in the world." I paused and looked back at Jimmy Lee and grinned. "The snipe," I said turning back to face the aliens.

"No! That's too dangerous even for them," Jimmy Lee said. "The last time I went out hunting a snipe, I almost didn't make it back."

The one in charge of the group of aliens snorted. "We have studied this planet for many cycles and do not know this snipe of which you speak." It stepped forward and watched me with large yellow eyes. Ned's comparison to a talking gator was seeming more and more appropriate. I was just glad the thing was talking and not shooting. If I could keep its interest, then we might have a chance.

"Not many people know bout the snipe. It is so elusive it can only be hunted by a group of at least...." I paused as I counted the aliens. "A group of ten beings." I hoped there weren't no more on the ship.

The alien glanced around at its companions then back at us. "It is fortunate you three are here then, as that makes the required number needed. It is also most interesting that that is the required number."

I nodded, ignoring the sharp teeth glistening in the alien's mouth as it looked at me. "It is indeed fortunate. And there is a lair not far from here where snipes can occasionally be caught off guard."

"And how does one hunt this dangerous snipe?" One of the guards moved away from the ship.

"They are hunted easily enough, *if* you can find them. You find one of their runs and position one person at the end with a large sack. The rest make their way to the other end of the run and walk back. When we scare up the snipe, we chase it down the run to the one holding the sack."

"If they are so easy to hunt, why do you need such a large number?"

"Ah, you see, you need at least nine people chasing them, that way theys don't turn around and attack," Jimmy Lee said. "We only had six on my last snipe hunt and the thing turned back to attack us instead of running. I's the only one made it back alive."

"This makes no sense," the other guard said. "If they are so powerful, how does the person waiting for them manage to capture them in a *sack*?"

"Well, ya see. By the time the snipe gets to the bag it is so tuckered out from running away it falls asleep in the bag. Still, the strongest member of the group should be the one left holding the bag." I grinned when I saw all the aliens looking toward the one that had come out of the ship. I had reckoned correctly.

"Uh, Billy Ray, which run were you thinking bout?" Jimmy Lee asked.

"The one over by the old Lafayette place."

Jimmy Lee gave me a wide-eyed stare as he took several steps back. "No way. That's the one we were hunting last time. I ain't going back there."

"Now, Jimmy Lee, we have these guys with us and we have the minimum number of hunters. We'll be alright." I glanced back over at the aliens. "However, that snipe does have a reputation of being one of the meanest in the area. Are there any more of you in that ship?"

"No." One of the aliens said.

I wasn't sure which one it was, though the leader snapped their head around and hissed something.

"Talking gators," Ned whispered.

"I ain't going," Jimmy Lee said again.

"I have no doubts my hunters can handle this snipe of yours. He can leave. If he is this frightened by it, he would be useless anyway."

I looked around at the other aliens, trying to look like I was studying them. I nodded as most them stood up straighter and shifted their weapons. "Perhaps you're right." I turned back to Jimmy Lee. "Seeing as how you're wanting to chicken out, maybe you'll at least escort our friend here to the western edge of the snipe run so he can set up."

"Sure. No problem. Come on, I'll show ya where they're gonna try and run that devil to ground at."

Jimmy Lee winked at me as he left. Old Man Lafayette was one of those paranoid, survivalist nuts, even before the war. Nowadays, he had that ravine and most of the area around his place booby trapped so well, even the coons had a hard time stealing from his trash. Jimmy Lee would alert Lafayette to what was going on and that would be the end of these talking gators. I wondered if there would be enough left of them to make a decent pair of boots.

~ * ~

It took the better part of an hour to reach the east end of the ravine. Them talking gators were complaining bout the water and they had all tripped at least once over a log or raised tree root. As we paused and surveyed the area, something moved in one of the shadows. One of the local cottontails raised its head to look at us.

"Snipe!" Ned raised his shotgun and fired. The buckshot peppered the area and the rabbit took off running—straight down the ravine—away from us.

"Don't let 'em get too far in front. They's be smart enough to set up ambushes." I stepped back as one of the aliens charged after the rabbit we had scared up.

Ned and I hung back as the rest of 'em began running after the "snipe". Like a gator, they were surprisingly fast as they moved. They didn't seem to notice we were no longer with them as they were caught up in the chase. Ned grinned and pointed to the side where the rabbit had stopped next to a large rock as the aliens ran past him. *No intelligent life on this planet? Maybe not, but we do have strong survival instincts round here,* I thought as I watched the rabbit crouched there, not moving, its eyes gleaming as they reflected the moonlight.

Ned held up his hand, his fingers raised in a silent countdown. At three we both ducked at the large explosion that came from further up the ravine and the rocks and debris that fell around us.

"Damn, I think Lafayette's been making his own gun powder again," Ned said.

A second explosion rocked the ground and we both turned and headed back home. We weren't too worried bout the ship seeing as how Lafayette would take care of it also. He wouldn't want anything brought here by aliens to be left behind to spy on him.

~ * ~

"Think any more of them talking gators will show up?" Jimmy Lee asked.

"I suppose it's possible they may come looking for the others, but if they do we can always take care of them as well." I propped my feet up on a nearby barrel and grinned as I crossed them; the dark leather of my new boots shimmered in the morning light.

Life in the Shadows

The sorceress paused as she passed through the mirrored hallway. *Strange*, she thought, glancing at her reflection. *I've never noticed this before.* On the wall behind her was a polished silver plate. With the mirror in front of her reflecting not only her image but also the one in the plate, the illusion of several versions of herself standing there was created.

As she watched, one of those images changed. Instead of her normal long black hair, this version had short red hair framing her heart shaped face. The clear violet eyes were the same and the silver shadowsilk gown still flowed over the same curves.

Desana blinked her eyes several times to clear the vision from her head. A flash of light reflecting from the mirror caused her to shut her eyes tightly.

Desana opened her eyes to find herself surrounded by a white wall covered with black runes. A loud tapping, like a thousand woodpeckers hitting the wall at the exact same time, filled her ears. The loudness of the tapping assaulted her senses and she fell to the ground. As the sound continued, she felt pressure building in her head, until it threatened to burst. A scream tore from her throat and she found herself sitting up in her bed.

"A dream? It was all just a dream?" she asked herself. Getting up she walked to her mirror to brush her hair, and stopped. The image that faced her had short red hair.

Desana dressed and hurried to her workroom. Her familiar, a small silver dragon, greeted her at the door. *Good morning, Misstresss. You sseem disstresssed thiss morning. What iss amisss?* The dragon watched her closely; his blue eyes wide with concern as he sent his thoughts.

"Good morning, Shesssian. Surely, you can see what is wrong. Look at my hair."

Your hair lookss jusst ass it alwayss hass.

Desana looked down at Shesssian and frowned. "Really, and what color is it?"

It iss the color of fire. It framess your face in the flamess of passsion.

"Prior to this morning, my hair has always been long and black. You once described it as a strand of midnight." Desana began pacing the room.

Honesstly, Misstresss, I do not remember that. Shesssian hopped up onto the worktable with a soft flutter of his wings.

"By the Lords of Chaos, the very fabric of reality has been altered. But, why didn't it alter my memories? Why do I still remember my hair being black? More importantly, what else has been changed that I don't know about?"

Desana walked over to one of her cluttered shelves and passed her hands over a large crystal ball. The sphere rose several inches off the shelf and hovered in front of the sorceress. Placing one hand an inch under the ball and the other an inch over, she guided the globe over to a silver stand on the worktable.

The globe settled gently onto the stand and flashed brightly. Desana passed her hands over the scrying crystal and spoke in a low murmuring voice. Inside the sphere, a rainbow of colors swirled. The colors slowly merged into a white paper, which floated in the globe. As she watched, Desana saw black marks appearing on the paper accompanied by the tapping from her dream.

What doess it mean? Shesssian asked.

"I don't know. I saw something similar to this in a dream last night." As she spoke, the tapping became louder. Desana began a series of complex gestures, and a shimmering surrounded her and Shesssian.

The sphere of protection created a reflective surface inside its walls and Desana again found herself studying an illusion created by reflections within reflections. After several minutes, the tapping stopped and she dismissed the shimmering ball.

Desana watched the reflected images fade, and frowned.

"Shesssian, you've walked on other planes of reality. Are there any that are like ours, but different?"

Yess, each time we make a decission that hass multiple optionss, ssomewhere another verssion of uss takess one of thosse other optionss. In ssome wayss each iss only a sshadow of the otherss.

"This is starting to make sense. In my dreaming last night, I must have stepped onto a crossroad of those realities. Somehow, details from this reality were transposed with those from another."

Desana picked up the scrying crystal and carried it back to the shelf. Before she could return it to its normal place, the tapping began again, and she dropped the globe, shattering it.

Turning, she watched as Shesssian faded from view, to be replaced by a black unicorn standing next to the table.

"Shesssian!"

The unicorn nodded his head, dipping a silver horn in acknowledgment.

~ * ~

"Karlie, did you get those changes I requested done?"

"Yes, Brian. Desana is now a redhead and instead of a miniature dragon for a familiar, she has a unicorn. I don't understand why you wanted the changes though."

"Oh, come on. All your heroines lately have had long black hair and all your sorcerers and sorceress's have had some kind of dragon as a familiar. It was long past time for a change."

"All right. Here you go." Karlie picked up the manuscript for her latest novel, *Life in the Shadows,* and handed it to her editor.

As Brian left the room, Karlie glanced at the dragon picture hanging next to the door, and saw herself reflected in its mirrored surface. This imagine also reflected the one from the mirror behind her, creating an infinite number of Karlies staring at her. Outside, a woodpecker began his rhythmic tapping.

The Final Blessing

After the Gods created Man, they gave him Woman to be his friend and companion as he journeyed through life. To woman they gave a chest containing blessings for her descendants. Woman was told never to open the chest, lest these precious gifts escape. Curiosity finally led Woman to open the chest and the divine blessings were lost—all but one.

~ * ~

Elpis shook his silver mane as darkness surrounded him. How long had it been since he had last been called? As the first born of those who guarded the final blessing of the gods he was only summoned when there seemed to be nothing left but defeat and despair. There were other guardians in the mortal realms; they were the ones who should be answering the normal calls. He stepped onto the ancient path and felt the ground pull at his hooves and the air grow heavy with the despair calling to him. When the darkness cleared, he found himself standing on a beach. He tossed his head and a golden glow from his horn surrounded him, pushing back the chill that hung like the touch of death. The stench of rotting bodies mixed with the salt spray of the ocean, creating a palpable fog. Red tinged water swirled around his hooves as he carefully followed the call that brought him here.

He stepped around a large outcropping of rocks and saw a man sleeping next to a small fire. He stepped closer and lay down beside the man. The ornateness of the man's armor and sword, which lay under his right hand, indicated he was a person of some importance in this place and time. Elpis studied the rugged face for a moment, noting the streaks where tears had flowed during the man's dreams.

He bowed his head, and gently, as to not wake him, touched the man's forehead with his horn. With practiced ease he entered the man's thoughts and began drawing the despair from his soul.

~ * ~

Odysseus shook his head as he surveyed the battle area. Bodies of both Greek and Trojan warriors lay together on the blood-stained sand. In death, their differences appeared to vanish. He wondered how many would meet as companions in the Elysium Fields of the afterlife.

The leader of the Greek armies turned toward the ocean to hide the tears he felt burning a path down his face. He refused to leave the area until the last Greek soldier's body was collected and prepared for the funeral rites tonight. *So many lives*, he thought. And, for what? Is one woman worth such a high price? It was a question he had heard many asking each other as well as in prayer to the Gods. The Gods, of course, refused to answer. After all, men were nothing more than playthings for their amusement.

He turned and glanced back at the high walls surrounding the city of Troy. Her defenders alert in their observation of the activity on the beach. Despite the temporary cease-fire to collect the bodies, it wouldn't take much to start another deadly rain of arrows from those walls. His men had found no way into the city and by now, most of them knew that was the only way they were going to defeat the Trojans and return Helen to her husband Menelaus. There had been discussion before this last battle of quitting the field and returning home. Something Odysseus had strongly opposed, but was now beginning to accept.

Odysseus felt something bump his back and he spun around, his hand going to his sword. There was nothing and no one there. He looked down at the ground and noticed a single print; small and delicate, but similar to a horse's hoof. He stared at the print for several minutes. Could the solution be something as simple as this? And it did seem so very simple. After so long on the field, with so many dead it seemed unlikely, but there was something about that single print in the sand. He glanced back at the walls of the city and nodded. The Trojans claimed Poseidon as their patron and the horse was sacred to the Sea God. Perhaps there was a way to breach those walls after all.

~ * ~

Elpis woke suddenly. A shrill neigh pierced the stillness of his grove then ended abruptly. He felt his heart tighten in a grip colder that the touch of Nyx herself. The area of the call was close to

17

where he had visited before. But, this time it wasn't the defeat of a single individual that was calling him, it was stronger; it was the despair of many. He stood and reared, neighing a challenge into the wind; calling for the one who guarded the gift for the city now buried in fear and defeat. It was a call that was not returned as it should have been.

The unicorn neighed again and stepped into the darkness that now hung before him. He found himself standing in a walled city, people running in different directions, fires dancing brightly. His nostrils burned from the smoke filling the city and his ears were deafened by the screams of the dying.

A man with a brightly polished sword stepped in front of him, not seeing him. Elpis snorted and took a startled step back. It was the same man he had visited before. The one whose sense of defeat had called him to this area. The one to whom he had brought the gift. Elpis felt his knees buckle and he dropped to the ground. Slowly, he bowed his head and touched the blood-stained ground with his horn in silent benediction to the unicorn who had once been the guardian of this now lost city. The most precious of the gods' gifts, hope, had been abused and was now gone from this place.

~ * ~

Elpis fought against the despair that threatened to engulf him as the death scream of another unicorn echoed in his soul. The screams had been coming more frequently over the centuries and he had lost count of the number of times he had heard that shrill neigh. Each time he thought he was ready for the pain, but he never was. How can one be prepared for the pain involved with losing a part of one's self—a part of one's own soul?

This time was the worst. It felt as if the pain from all the previous deaths had been multiplied together. He tried to neigh his challenge, but fell to the ground, his legs too weak to support him. His vision blurred, and then all he could see were swirling lights. His breathing became labored and he gasped, trying to keep his lungs functioning. He felt his heart drumming erratically; desperately trying to escape the confines of his chest.

He closed his eyes and forced himself to take long deep breaths. He fought for a semblance of calm until the pain passed.

He got slowly to his feet, his legs still shaking, his body trembling. Elpis shook himself and a spray of water fell from his body. He raised his head and neighed a weak challenge to the cloud of despair that hung over his grove. As the blackness thickened, Elpis took a deep breath and once again stepped onto the ancient path.

The unicorn had to fight for every step he took on the path. The ground protested loudly as he pulled each hoof free from its grasp. The weight of the air tried to force the breath from his lungs and push him to the ground with each agonizing step.

Loud explosions in the distance accompanied a sudden call of despair deeper than that, which had brought him here originally.

~ * ~

Elpis paused and looked around, each time he was called to the mortal realms it seemed to have changed in significant ways. Tall buildings reached up to grasp at the sky and the hard, black surface of the ground was covered in thick dust, twisted pieces of metal, broken buildings and shattered glass. Elpis stepped carefully through the debris. He briefly touched noses with one of the search dogs who was standing with his head hung and his eyes glazed as he stared at the area. As he walked away, Elpis heard a sharp bark from the dog. He turned to see the rescue team pull a young child from the rubble. He stopped and looked up at the thick black smoke from the explosion that had wrought this destruction and felt the despair that hung over this city. His knees buckled as the weight of it pressed down on him.

The unicorn fell to the debris-strewn ground, unable to move. He was only one: The last of the ancient guardians. In a world filled with sorrow, hatred, fear and their related emotions, he was the only bringer of hope left.

A ghostly shape appeared before him. It was a woman carrying a black box with the symbols of the most ancient Gods carved on it. She smiled sadly, her eyes downcast, as she slowly opened the box. From its depths, small globes of darkness flew out and surrounded the fallen unicorn. Elpis tried to stand, but the darkness blanketed him, and trapped him in its cold embrace.

He looked up to see the woman close the box then reach out to grasp his horn. "I give you that which I have protected since the beginning. I give you the last gift." At her touch, the blanket of darkness sank into his body. Elpis shuddered as he fought against the pain and coldness that invaded his heart and soul. As suddenly as the despair had touched him, it vanished.

Elpis felt warmth grow in his soul and begin to swell outward. A golden glow surrounded him and burst over the area. He reared up and neighed his challenge to the despair that hung over the city.

A soft whinny caught his attention, and he turned his head slowly to see a woman pick up and embrace the girl rescued from the rubble only moments before. At the woman's side was a unicorn.

Tears filled his eyes, and through their glittering curtain, Elpis began to see more shimmering shapes as they began to take on the forms of silver-maned, golden-horned unicorns. As the unicorns began to spread out through the area, Elpis watched as people began to search again with a new sense of purpose. People turned to strangers to offer words of comfort and encouragement or just simply a place to cry.

Elpis neighed again, his voice filled with joy; not challenge. His call was joined by a multitude of other neighs that echoed through the air. Gradually, other golden glows spread over the area and the despair began loosening its stranglehold on the city. This was one city that would not be lost. From this place, hope would again find its way into the hearts of man. The greatest gift of the Gods was reborn in the world.

The Sword of Power

The Sword of Power is given to heal and unify—not to hack and divide.

"Have you heard?" a soft, melodic male voice asked, startling Viviane out of her meditations.

The High Priestess of Avalon composed herself then stood and faced the speaker. "I have," she said, studying her visitor. He was an older man dressed in a tattered brown traveling cloak. In the shadows of his hood, his sharp blue eyes sparkled with the strength of his soul. His name was Talisen, but he was more properly called by his title: Merlin. As the Chief Druid of Breton, his position was almost equal to her own.

Viviane gestured to the stone benches that ringed the meditation grove. The Merlin nodded, took a seat on the nearest bench and pushed his hood back revealing his lined face, graying hair and beard. She sat next to him.

"We both knew Uther was not the one. Yet you gave him the sword anyway," Viviane said.

"The land needed a king and the sword accepted Uther. Healing has begun."

"Only to be stopped now; at the time of his death. He has no acknowledged heir—only a bastard son whom the dukes will not accept. If he is able to claim his father's throne, he may be the one. Until that time though, the land is again without a king."

"There is another problem. The sword is missing." The Merlin looked in the direction of the Goddess' Well.

"What?" Viviane's cry echoed across the grove and several of the novice priestesses turned to look at her and the Merlin before returning to their meditations.

Viviane stood and turned away from the Merlin to glance at the novices finishing their morning meditations. Each year the number of girls chosen by the Goddess grew smaller and smaller. Avalon was being supplanted as those who followed the Christ continued to force their faith on others. Avalon had already slipped into another realm and only through the power of the

21

Goddess could it be reached at all. Eventually that power would fade and Avalon would be cut off from the mortal world. If that happened, the power of the Goddess would also fade from the world.

The sword had been created with the power of the Goddess. For centuries, the High King had carried it as a symbol of the Goddess' protection of both the king and the land of which he was a part. *If the sword is gone does that mean the Goddess' protection is gone as well?*

"Lady Viviane," one of the younger priestess called, running into the grove. "The well...the well...the waters of the well."

"I am called." Viviane left the Merlin standing alone in the grove as she hurried to Goddess' Well.

Viviane knelt next to the Well and passed her hand over the sparkling, diamond surface of the well. A slight tingle passed through her as the power of the Goddess touched her. The dancing, shimmering surface smoothed to a glowing mirror, clouded for a moment, then cleared as the picture of a darkened room formed on the surface.

She felt a moment's disorientation then found herself standing in a corner of the dark room. A large stone table with a body laid on it stood before her. Candles placed at the head and foot of the table. The flickering light cast distorted shadows on the walls of the small room. Incense burned in braziers at the corners of the table, and Viviane wrinkled her nose at the cloying, sweet smell that filled the area.

Viviane shook her head; this was not a normal well vision. Those came as pictures in the water. This was the first time she had been pulled into a vision in this manner. Viviane relaxed and placed her trust in the Goddess who guided the vision.

She stepped over to look at the body. Dressed in his full battle armor, lay Uther, the Pendragon and High King of Breton. She stared at the body for a minute then turned her attention to the sword scabbard at his side. The red velvet, with the runes of power stitched in silver, looked faded and worn, but the feel of the Goddess' power was unmistakable. Her hand trembled as Viviane reached out and touched the empty scabbard. She fought the reaction to jerk her hand away from the surge of power she felt in that touch. *Where is the sword?*

Another flash of light and Viviane found herself back in the dark corner. She watched as Uther's body was brought into the room. Along with Igraine and the servants were several of the Christ's priests. They carefully arranged the body on the table, lit the candles and incense, then recited several prayers. After the servants left and most of the priests escorted Igraine from the room; one remained behind. "Uther Pendragon, you failed to stop the worship of false gods and this is your punishment," he said.

Viviane felt her anger building as she watched him remove the sword, place it under his robes and leave the room. *Do the followers of the Christ honestly expect to place one of their choosing on the throne? The Goddess will not allow the sword to be used in such a manner!*

Despite having been Ambrosias' choice as successor, it had still taken the sword for Uther to be accepted as High King. Merlin had given it to him in order to heal the land after decades of fighting among the various clans. The ploy had only worked for a short time. Uther was not the one destined to heal and unify, and the sword had refused to protect him when his own dukes set upon him from an ambush.

She slowly traced the silver runes with her fingers and felt the power drain from the scabbard. This was why the Goddess had brought her here: to show her the treachery of the followers of the Christ and to remove the Goddess' power from the scabbard. She, Viviane, Lady of the Lake and High Priestess of Avalon would have to recover the sword.

~ * ~

Viviane walked along the old paths. Here the veil separating Avalon from Glastonbury was thinnest. She listened carefully, and could hear the ringing of church bells as well as the singing of the priestesses of Avalon. Viviane found the blended harmony of the music to be a bit unsettling as she listened. The church bells and the song of the priestesses were very different melodies from two different worlds, separated by magic and their beliefs. To listen to the music separately, one would never think they could meld together as if parts of a whole. Yet here, at the veil, the two seemed to complement and speak to each other.

She stopped as a shimmering glow appeared before her. Through the veil, two images wavered then formed. First, she saw the Druid Circle, and then the church. Before the scene could change again, she stepped through and stood only a few yards from the church. The chill of the mists surrounded her like a shroud, the air cooler and heavier.

Viviane took a deep breath and called on the Goddess. She felt a renewed strength as the Goddess' power touched her.

~ * ~

Viviane looked around as she entered the church. She did not understand how the followers of the Christ could feel closer to their God inside closed walls. The dark room held rows of wooden benches in front of a dais. Hung on the wall behind the dais was a large wooden cross with the figure of a man on it and beneath it stood a table with several candles. One of the priests was there lighting the candles. Viviane sneezed as the heavy, sweet incense in the air burned her nostrils.

The tall, gray haired priest turned from the candles and nodded politely. "Lady Viviane," he said. "Why do you come here?"

"Father Gregory, I am here to reclaim the property of Avalon. The sword must be returned to the Goddess' keeping," Viviane said.

"If it were in my power, I would return the sword to you. The Abbot, however, has claimed the sword in the name of the Church."

"And, there it will remain," a portly man said, as he entered the sanctuary. He grasped the gold crucifix on the chain around his neck with his left hand then crossed himself as he glared at Viviane.

"By what right do you claim that which belongs to Avalon?" Viviane demanded.

The Abbot frowned and crossed his arms over his chest. "If the sword is the property of Avalon, as you say, then why is the symbol of the Grail upon it?"

Viviane sneered at the Abbot. "It is the symbol of the Goddess' Well, not the Cup!"

"Excuse me, Lady Viviane," Father Gregory said, stepping forward. "It is the Grail symbol. I have seen Avalon's symbol for the Goddess' Well and this is different."

"That proves the sword now belongs to the one true God;

not your false Goddess," the Abbot said, smiling.

"I wish to see this change for myself!" Viviane took a deep breath and forced herself to meet the Abbot's challenging look with one of calm reserve.

The Abbot glanced at Father Gregory and shook his head. Father Gregory ignored the implied command. "If you'll follow me," he said, gesturing to a small doorway to the side.

Viviane stopped when she stepped through the door and saw the sword gleaming in the candlelight next to a simple clay cup. With a nod of obeisance to the power she felt resonating between the two relics, Viviane stepped forward and picked up the sword. There on the metal, next to the hilt, she found the Grail symbol, just as the Abbot had claimed.

She glanced up and saw the smug expression on the Abbot's face and a curious one on Father Gregory's. Viviane turned the blade in her hands and smiled when she saw the Goddess' emblem on the other side. The two symbols were very similar. Both were cups, however, where the Cup of the Well held the crescent moon of the Goddess, the Grail had a cross.

She gripped the hilt of the sword in her right hand then raised both arms as she called the mists. Now, that she held the sword it would be a simple matter of passing through the veil and returning to Avalon.

As the mists filled the room, Viviane again heard the blended harmony of the church bells and the priestess's song. She glanced at the Abbot and Father Gregory. Neither had moved since she called the mists. Both stood watching her, their eyes and faces blank. As they grew, the mists did not have their familiar feel as they surrounded her. Though she felt the usual tingle of power, she also felt an unusual warmth in the contact.

When the mists cleared, she found herself next to the Goddess' Well and the water appeared to boil in anger. She knelt and passed her hand over the surface. The waters stilled and she studied the image that formed.

A group of druids stood in a circle around a mound of dirt. *A grave?* Viviane wondered. One of the druids stepped out of the circle, placed a plain clay cup on the mound, and raised his arms to the sky. "The many are one," he said.

The many are one. Viviane heard the Goddess' voice repeating the words of the druid in her mind. Again, the blended harmony of the bells and song echoed in her soul.

"The many are one," Viviane whispered softly, as the church reappeared around her.

The Abbot blinked several times then shook his head and asked. "What was that?"

"Something the Goddess just reminded me of. The many are one." Viviane turned away from the Abbot to face Father Gregory. "You were correct, the Well symbol has changed into the Grail, yet the symbol of the Goddess remains on the other side. Doubtless, it is a sign that the one who will wield the sword must be willing to recognize both the Goddess and the Christ, just as the Druids once did."

"No!" The Abbot reached out to take the sword from her. As his hand grasped the blade, a bright flash of light filled the room.

~ * ~

This time Viviane did not travel alone. Both the abbot and priest stood on either side of her and looked upon an unlikely scene. The Grail rested on the freshly dug mound from Viviane's previous vision while six Druids called forth its power and melded it with the power of the dragon. A heavy mist filled the area as they chanted. "Unal nathtrac uthras bethid dothyel denvey."

When the chant ended, and the mist cleared, she could see a pair of large stones now stood in front of each of the six Druids. The blue tinted stones glowed softly, the same as the Cup.

"Now, you see why Avalon and Glastonbury exist side by side. It was the power of both which raised the Druid Circle," Viviane whispered.

"I have seen no Druid Circle. I do not accept the illusions of a witch as evidence," the Abbot protested.

Viviane looked directly into the Abbot's gray eyes and spoke softly. "Are you secure enough in your faith to accompany me to Avalon?"

The Abbot turned a deep crimson as he looked at her. "What of the sword? Do you believe I am such a fool I would allow you to take it into your realm?"

Viviane sighed softly then glanced at the priest. "Let Father Gregory carry the sword. He is a true man of faith. Avalon trusts his honor."

Viviane frowned at the anger in the look the Abbot gave Father Gregory, but said nothing more as she waited for his answer.

"Very well, I agree," the Abbot finally said.

Viviane nodded and the trio found themselves returned once more to the sanctuary of the church. She raised her hands and began calling the mists. As High Priestess, Viviane knew she could have led them along the old paths, but felt a display of the Goddess' powers on the sanctified land of the Christ would be more impressive. As the mists dissipated, the church faded and they found themselves standing inside the Druid Circle of their vision. In front of them stood a stone slab, several symbols carved into the top. Most prominent was the dragon as it curled protectively around the Grail. Above the dragon was the crescent moon of the Goddess.

"Joseph of Arimathaea's grave," Viviane whispered reverently. "The Druids consecrated the ground in the names of the Goddess and the Christ when they buried him here. This is one of the holiest places in Avalon, and the focal point that joins Avalon with your world. Just as the land and the king are one; so too are the many incarnations of the divine by which man interprets the world." Viviane reached down and laid her hand on the crescent moon carved on the stone.

"The druids took in a weary Joseph of Arimathaea and cared for him. They accepted his faith as his own and did not try to force theirs on him. He told them tales of the Christ and they recognized him as another aspect of the Horned King, the Goddess' consort who sacrifices himself for his land and his people."

The Abbot grabbed her shoulders and turned Viviane toward him. "How dare you speak such blasphemies!"

"Blasphemy!" Viviane jerked away from the Abbot. "I have felt the hand of my Goddess and have heard her voice speak to me. For you to deny the existence of other powers is the blasphemy. Even your scriptures admit to the existence of other Gods. Have you never read them?" Viviane asked.

"Lady Viviane, I don't believe you intended to turn this into a theological debate. We should return to the issue at hand; the sword, and to whom it rightfully belongs," Father Gregory said, resting the sword on the stone covering the grave.

The point of the sword touched the crescent moon of the Goddess and Viviane felt a surge of power in the air. For a brief moment, the church and the Druid Circle seemed to merge into one place.

In this new vision a group of clerics stood inside the Druid Circle along with the Druids from the earlier vision. From among the clerics one stepped forward and removed his vestments, exchanging them for the somber robe of The Merlin.

"Talisen's predecessor as Merlin of Breton." Viviane said. "During his time it was believed important for the one who held the position to learn about all the faiths of the people," Viviane said.

As they continued to watch, one of the priests, the Abbot of that time to judge by his elaborate clothing, held the Grail out to the Merlin, who drank deeply from it. "For many years, the Cup was used to anoint the new Merlin, the High Priestess of Avalon and the Abbot of Glastonbury. It bound them in their oaths to guide and protect the people in all their faiths. It is only recently that those oaths have not been enforced by Avalon or the Church," Viviane said.

She turned and looked at the Abbot and was surprised at the thoughtful expression on his face as he watched the scene before them. *Perhaps there is hope for Avalon,* she thought.

The veil separating Avalon from the mortal world was getting harder to pass through each year. Viviane knew it would not be long before it proved impossible to breach and Avalon would vanish from this reality completely. If the next High King were bound to Avalon then perhaps that day would not come as quickly.

Again, the vision faded and Viviane found herself standing next to the Abbot in the Druid Circle. The cold breeze pricked at her skin with needles of ice. A sudden pain in her heart caused her to gasp aloud. The Abbot reached out to support her and she felt a brief tingle of warmth at his contact. "The dragon," she said softly. "The sword?"

"Lady Viviane, the stone holds the sword, I cannot remove it," Father Gregory said.

Viviane stared at the sword where it now stood trapped in the burial stone. The point had pierced the crescent moon of the

Goddess and approximately half of the blade was buried in the stone. She placed a trembling hand on the stone and called upon the Goddess. For several minutes, she stood there, but received no answer to her question.

"With this sword Uther was able to secure his kingship. It is only with this sword that the next king will be accepted. Let the sword decide who is to be king," Viviane said finally.

"Let it be as God wills," Father Gregory said.

"No!" The Abbot slammed his hands against the stone. "This cannot be. This is all an illusion."

"Perhaps you would care to remove the sword yourself." Viviane smiled, gestured to the sword, and stepped away from the stone.

The Abbot nodded and shoved Father Gregory aside as he stepped around and reached for the sword. There was a spark as his hand touched the hilt and his face twisted as he fought to remove it from the stone. After several minutes, he finally released the sword. "I cannot," he said between breaths. "I do not know what magic you have cast here, but I will see the spell broken and the sword reclaimed in the name of the one true God."

"That is a matter for your God and the Goddess to decide," Viviane said. She raised her arms and again called the mists. When they cleared, the trio stood in the small churchyard. There in front of the church they found a large rock with the sword firmly embedded in it, much like the one in Avalon. "The one who is able to draw the sword will have to penetrate the veil between Glastonbury and Avalon to grasp the sword properly. Only if he can reach into both realms will he be able to remove the sword from the stone."

Viviane nodded respectfully to the Abbot and Father Gregory, then turned to leave. She walked carefully back along the path she had followed to the church. After passing through the veil, she turned and looked back towards the church. She nodded when she saw the sword appear in both Avalon and Glastonbury. The shifting scene confirmed what she told the Abbot. The one to wield Excalibur, the sword of power, must be willing to accept both the Goddess and the Christ.

As she continued to watch the shifting scene, time moving differently through the veil, she saw a young man reaching for the sword. "Arthur," she said softly, "the son of Uther and Igraine." She bowed her head respectfully as the sword came free of the stone and the scene faded.

The Asylum Wall

There is nothing here, I think as I clutch the papers I'm carrying tighter to my chest then force my eyes up from the walkway to look at the building. *Nothing except ghosts and memories.*

It has only been a few years since the place closed, but it looks like it has been abandoned for decades. Almost all of the small windows are broken, giving the building a pot marked appearance in the light of an early twilight. The doors hang crooked in their frames and weeds have overrun the once smooth lawn. The place is dead and only the ghosts and memories remain.

I take a breath and push open the arching main gates; their grinding and squeaking echoes in the silence of the area. "Ghosts can't hurt you," I whisper as the echoes fade.

Broken asphalt shifts and crunches under my feet. Up close, the decay is even more obvious. Deep wrinkles and creases line the front of the building where the paint is cracked and peeling. Moss hangs from the eaves, veiling and shadowing the broken, empty windows. I reach for the partially open door and step through, back into the memories I came here to face.

Dust covers everything in the entry hall and I swallow the cough scratching at the back of my throat. As I walk through the lobby, the dust swirls around me creating mists and vapors that bring memories of the people who once worked or lived here back into sharp focus. I am reminded of the doctors and nurses— some of whom were easy to work with and were still fresh enough they hadn't become cynical or callous. There were others who had worked with our patients far too long and had begun to expect the worse behavior from them or had to have it proven which ones weren't BiFFs, or Big Fat Fakers. We did receive a percentage of those as well. Shadowy forms also became some of the patients I had worked with over the years. There—a young man in his late twenties physically, but maybe four or five mentally and emotionally. He used to follow everyone around like a little puppy. We could never get him to keep his shoes on. I smile as I remember how he used to carry a security blanket with him. Fortunately, one of the other, more stable patients would always seem to adopt him and make sure he stayed out of trouble.

The ghostly figure shifts and I stepped back as one of the BiFFs jumps toward me—a young woman who had been ordered here, several times, from one of the county jails, for evaluation. I didn't know her charges; I was never curious about that sort of thing as I felt it would prejudice my attitude when I dealt with our high security patients. This one though, she was a classic. She wanted to make you think she was crazy, but you could see the calculating going on in her head. Some nights she would create as many disturbances as she could; getting all the other patients on the floor upset and agitated. Then some days she would go into a sweet little girl act, being polite and helpful and other times, she just became as disgusting as she thought she could away with.

We all knew she was a behavior issue and after a few days, the doctors would release her back to the county jail. But, she knew the right buttons to push each time she went to court to make the judge think she honestly had mental health issues and each time he would order her back here for an evaluation. I always suspected the officers at the jail appreciated the break they got when she was with us. Considering the way we felt after dealing with her, I couldn't blame them.

As I leave the lobby and enter the patient areas, the dust thickens and I find myself walking in a dense fog that obscures my vision. Still I know where I am going and only pause to nod a greeting to each of my memories as we pass.

My hand shakes as I reach for the door to this room. A spark arcs from the knob to my hand, flashing bright blue and creating a halo of light in the fog. The bluish glow surrounds the door as I step through and back into my past.

*

"Deirdre, we just got a call from the sheriff's dispatcher," Marco said as he stepped out of the office. "They picked up some guy wandering around downtown in robes, carrying a staff and talking about dragons chasing him. They'll be bringing him in on an M-One hold for evaluation." He handed her some papers.

"Did they say how long?" Deirdre looked up and pushed her

glasses up on her nose as she glanced at the papers.

Marco looked at his watch. "Should be here in about five minutes. Which room?"

"Let's use room ten."

"I'll get it ready. Let me know when they get here."

"Sure."

Deirdre Ashlyn closed the word processing file she had been working on and pulled up the admittance files and started entering the preliminary information from the notes Marco had handed her.

"Where do you want us to put Gandalf here?"

Deirdre looked up from the computer to see two deputies standing at the desk. She shook her head. Tom had never learned to use any of the verbal judo skills she knew his office taught. "Marco should have room ten ready."

She nodded toward the staff the other deputy was holding. "Is that it for his property?" She held her hand out for it.

"We didn't find anything else on the initial pat down," the young man said handing her the staff.

Deirdre took the gnarled wood and gasped as an electric shock went through her arm.

"Are you okay?" Tom grabbed the staff.

"No!" The old man in the robes stepped toward Tom. "That is not for you. You must give it back to the one who has been chosen."

"It's okay," Deirdre said pulling the staff back. She smiled at the younger deputy, who had placed a hand on the old man's shoulder, but had not thrown him on the floor or into a wall as others would have done.

"Come on old man, let's get you to your room," Marco said.

"I still need a name for the records," Deirdre said.

The old man looked at her, his gray eyes glowing in the dim lighting of the area. "You may call me Brayden."

"Is that your first or last name?" She found herself staring at his eyes.

"Just Brayden." He turned toward Marco. "I believe you said you had a room waiting for me."

"This way." Marco gestured down the hall.

Deirdre watched them as they walked away from her desk.

Just a coincidence, she thought as she went back to filling out the forms.

~ * ~

A sharp pain stabs my hand, the same as I felt the first time I touched Brayden's staff, and I shudder as the electric shock pulses through my body. Even now, I know the name he gave me was only a coincidence, but a part of me wants to believe it wasn't.

As I look around the room, the dust begins to settle on the walls and words start to form on the white paint. I close my eyes for a moment. When I open them, the words are still there—clearer. I stare at the walls and realize that unlike the rest of the building, the walls in this room are still stark white and smooth. The letters seem to shimmer for a moment then swirl and shift. Here and there, I see lines and passages I recognize from some of the stories I had written.

Brayden was a writer also. He would spend hours scribbling on the walls of his room at night. Then when all of the space was covered, he would clean the walls and start over. I remember asking him what he was writing about once and he turned to me, his gray eyes as dark as storm clouds. "The same thing you are." He smiled then turned back to the wall. "I am looking for a way back to where I belong; while you are looking for the place where you belong. We will both get there one day—through our magic and words."

"Magic," I asked.

"Magic." He smiled as he looked at me. "Stories are a form of magic. Through them you create worlds and people. There are writers who are able to breath true life into their worlds and transport others into them. These worlds really do exist and sometimes they intersect with this one."

I laughed at the image I suddenly had of a unicorn trotting down a street.

"Do not laugh. Bards have always created worlds of wonder for others. Some of these worlds are small and only a handful ever visit, they only linger for a short time, before they are forgotten and fade into mist. But others become a part of the background of this place. They are the repository of the magic your world wants to believe in, but your science refuses to recognize. The more people visit a world; either by reading the creative words of the writer or by daydreaming about it—the longer it will last."

He turned back to the wall and placed his hand on it—sliding his fingers under the words he had written before I came in.

"Sometimes there is enough power in the words that a chosen few can actually cross over and enter the world."

At that point, he started writing again and I decided it was time to leave.

That night when I went home, I found Brayden's staff sitting in the corner of the small room I used as an office. I stared at it for a few minutes then sat at my computer and began typing.

I had had an idea for a fantasy novel for a number of years and while I had sketched out a general outline and knew who my main character was, I hadn't done much work on it in several months. Tonight though was different, I read through the notes I had on the story and on the character I had named Brayden, before I ever met the one I now knew as a harmless but delusional old man, and began typing. I didn't stop typing until I heard the alarm in my bedroom go off, informing me it was time to get up and get ready for work.

I glanced at the staff still sitting in the corner; there seemed to be a soft glow surrounding it. "Good, you have opened the door," I heard Brayden's voice whisper behind me.

My head jerked up and I found myself sitting in my bed—alarm still buzzing. Had it all been a dream? I thought so at the time. When I checked my computer before leaving for work, I found a new file in the folder where my writing projects were stored. This one though was password protected, and I didn't know the password. I started to delete the file, but stopped as I looked up at the place the staff had been—there was nothing there now. *Time for a vacation, Deidre,* I told myself. *You've been working with some of these people so long you're starting to have hallucinations.*

~ * ~

"Hey, you feeling okay?" Marco asked causing Deidre to jerk her head up.

"Been fighting a headache for the last hour or so," she said.

Marco frowned. "You take anything?"

"Aspirin. It's not helping."

"Don't go getting sick on me; it's just the two of us tonight so you can't go home."

"I know. Tonight's my Friday; I should be able to make it till the end of shift."

"That's the spirit. Hang in there."

"Thanks." Deirdre watched Marco walk down the hall to check on the patients.

"He's cleaning his wall again," Marco said when he came back to the desk.

"You might want to make a note on that." Deirdre looked up and frowned. "The walls weren't even a quarter full this morning."

Marco nodded the headed for the small office.

She waited a few minutes then got up and walked down the hallway and paused at Brayden's room. "It's time for the story to be finished," she heard him say. She looked through the small window and saw him sitting on the floor, staring at some papers in his lap. There were several others scattered on the floor around him.

She shook her head and went back to her desk.

~ * ~

A sudden chill causes me to shiver in the room as I remember the scene. Looking down at the floor, I see a stray piece of paper and reach down to pick it up. There is something written on it, but it has faded to a pale gray that almost blends with the paper. I squint and angle the paper to better catch the little light coming in through the small window. "How?" I gasp as I drop the paper.

I glance at the stack of papers I had placed on the old mattress. The only words on the top page *Sylvan Shadows*, stare up at me as I reached for the dropped paper. The words on the page are the same. *Sylvan Shadows*.

"Brayden!" I yell in the silence.

The only reaction I get is dust swirling around me.

The dust begins to settle and my mind again sees Brayden sitting on the floor with his papers. We had found him in the same position that morning at breakfast. Both Marco and I had thought he had been reading during the night and hadn't disturbed him. However, that morning we discovered he was dead.

There was nothing to indicate how he had died; it was as if

his spirit had just left his body. I remembered seeing a slight glow, like a doorway, on the wall, but no one else acted as if they had seen it so I never mentioned it.

I quit working here about a month after Brayden died, I also stopped writing for a while. There was something about his death that rattled me; it was as if I could feel his spirit watching me, just as I felt he was here with me now. About six months after I quit, his staff reappeared in my apartment and I found my desire to write had also returned. *Sylvan Shadows* was the result of that return to writing and it featured a harmless, but slightly delusional old wizard named Brayden.

Now, only a few years since that night, they closed the hospital about a year later, something has led me back here. Something that was telling me to bring this copy of the story here for Brayden. I place the faded page on top of my stack and smile. He once told me he was writing the same thing I was. Perhaps there was some kind of weird psychic connection between us. Maybe there was something to his comments about writers creating worlds with their words. Or perhaps, I had unconsciously plagiarized what he had been writing on the walls when he was here.

"Deirdre."

I jump and turn toward the soft voice. A glowing figure stands in front of a doorway in the wall.

"Brayden?"

"Yes." He holds out his hand. "I was able to open the portal that night and leave your world and return to my own. Stealing your creativity was the only way I could touch any form of magic in this world. Now that you have again found your muse, and your magic, I would invite you to come to my world."

"Would I ever be able to return?"

"Unlikely."

I look past his shoulder and saw the world I had created in my fantasy novel and some other stories. A place that was young and green. A world of magic and wonder. A place I had desired to be for a long time.

I nod and take his hand. There is a sudden spark of electricity, like when I opened the door to the room. It then wraps around my wrist in a glowing band.

"Look," Brayden says nodding toward something behind me.

I turn and see my body sitting on the floor against the bed—just as his had been that night. The copy of my manuscript still neatly stacked on the mattress. I smile as I realize *Sylvan Shadows* will probably be a bestseller for my agent, with the added mystique of my mysterious death in the mental hospital I used to work at. I'm sure one of the other former employees will tell someone about the last patient to be housed in room ten as well. And the story of the old man named Brayden who thought he was a wizard from another world will only add to the popularity of the story—keeping it and this world alive for a long time.

The Gift of All

Okay, I'm tired of it. The Patriarchal religions and governments have for too long made me out to be the cause of all Man's woes and I'm sick of it. Now before you think, I'm just another feminist standing on her soapbox, I should tell you who I am. My name is Pandora. Sound familiar? I have also been called Eve and a host of other names. In essence, I was the first woman created by God, Goddess, or the Gods depending on your religious beliefs. However, no matter what your specific beliefs, if you were raised in one of the Patriarchal religions, then you've heard the story about how Woman caused the fall of Man.

Of course, I haven't always been as bitter as I am now. This is something that has built over the centuries as the stories have propagated and been adapted by other cultures to fit their own world view and religious bias. Despite my personal feelings, I will try to tell my story without sarcasm and bitterness, but I make no guarantees that I will succeed.

Let's start with the Greeks, since I'm in my guise as Pandora. Depending on how this goes, I might tell you my feelings on that blasted snake and the apple as well. However, as I said we will start with the Greeks and that means telling my version of the story about that trice-damned box and how it is my fault Man has been plagued with sorrow since I was created. Yeah. Right. Sorry, sarcasm again. Let me take a breath and calm myself then I'll begin.

~ * ~

My first memories are of waking on a soft bed, dressed in a blue silk gown, my hair long and as black as the cloak of Nyx herself. The marble of the floor sent a chill through my body when my bare feet touched it. With no walls to block my passage, I left the room. From that first room I moved between columns of white marble and passed through several others; similarly laid out, finally entering a large chamber dominated by two thrones and an obsidian table.

Looking down at the smooth surface of the table, I saw my features reflected in its black surface. My skin was pale and smooth. My eyes appeared to be blue, the same color as my gown. My mind searched for the name that belonged to the face floating in the darkness, none appeared. My hand reached out to touch the image and I felt warmth where there should have been none.

How long I stared at my reflection, I do not remember. Suddenly the image wavered and vanished. I straightened and turned slowly around, before me stood several men and women. Those faces, my mind was able to give names to: Zeus, Hera, Apollo, Artemis, Athena, Ares, Hades and several others. Zeus and his wife, Hera, stepped away from the group and seated themselves on the two thrones.

I dropped to one knee and bowed my head before the King and Queen of the heavens.

"Proceed," I heard Zeus say. His voice rumbled throughout the building and I felt the marble under me quiver.

I didn't move as the others approached me. Their sandaled feet passed me slowly and I felt them lay their hands on my head before they moved away. At each touch, I felt something embrace me: A warm tingling sensation that was also chilling as it surrounded and penetrated my body.

Finally, Zeus and Hera stood and approached me. The King of the Gods reached down, grasped my arm lightly and gently guided me to my feet. Hera handed me a small black chest with the symbols of the gods inlayed in gold and silver across its surface. A simple clasp and chain secured the lid.

"You are Pandora," Zeus said, placing his hand on my shoulder. "And you will be the mother to the race of Man. Today the Gods have created you, and each has given you a gift. These gifts you will pass on to your children and they to theirs."

My hands trembled slightly as I touched the clasp on the box.

"The gifts I speak of were given to you directly; they are not contained there. You are given charge of that chest; to guard and protect it, however you are never to open it. If you do, you will condemn your children and those who follow them to sorrow and despair."

I was unable to respond. Even then I wondered why the

Gods would give me the chest if it was so dangerous. Why not keep it with them where it could remain secure? Surely, they didn't want to risk something evil being released into the world they had created.

Zeus gestured to his right and Hermes appeared next to him. "Hermes will conduct you to Epimetheus who will be your husband."

I should have realized something was wrong at that time. Epimetheus wasn't a mortal but was one of the Titans who preceded the time of the Olympians. He and his brother Prometheus sided with Zeus in his war against Cronos and, as a result, were not exiled to Tartarus with the others. Nevertheless, I didn't think about this then. I only smiled as Hermes took my arm and we vanished from Olympus.

We reappeared in front of a magnificent house. White columns surrounded the large open entryway and reminded me of the architecture of Olympus. Here the sun shone brightly and my feet warmed as I stood on the marble parch. Epimetheus and Prometheus were both waiting for us at the steps. Hermes bowed slightly as he stepped away from me. "May I present the Lady Pandora, a gift from the Gods of Olympus to Epimetheus," he said before vanishing.

I stood there as Epimetheus stepped forward. "Welcome, Lady Pandora."

"Thank you, Lord Epimetheus." It was the first words I had spoken and I was surprised at the soft melodic sound of my voice.

"Be careful, my brother. It would be foolish to trust Zeus," Prometheus said.

Epimetheus only nodded and continued to stare at me. I had seen my reflection in the obsidian table and knew I was fair. I also knew Aphrodite had blessed me with beauty and grace. It was doubtful Epimetheus had even heard his brother speaking.

Aphrodite, Goddess of Love and Beauty, whose gift was to beguile and seduce others and yet despite her divine abilities she had to rely on a magic girdle to augment her powers. Just how beguiling could she have been if she could not trust her own abilities and had to use an external device? Oops, sorry about that little ramble, back to my story.

Prometheus stepped forward and looked at the chest. "Is this also a gift from the Gods?"

I stepped back and turned to my right a little to shield the chest from the Titan. "It is mine."

Prometheus frowned then nodded and stepped back, his eyes never leaving the chest. Neither he nor Epimetheus ever asked about it again, not even after it was opened.

Epimetheus welcomed me into his home and for many years, we were very happy together. We had many daughters; all blessed with the gifts the Gods had given to me before I left Olympus. During all this time, the black chest sat in the storeroom where I had placed it. In time, I forgot about the thing as well as the warnings of Zeus.

Late one evening, an old woman came to my door requesting shelter during the night. It seemed strange to me that I did not know this woman, yet, my mind did not pursue the question of who she might be. Despite, my initial hesitation, I invited her in and prepared a large meal. Afterwards, I escorted her to one of the large bedrooms for the night.

Thinking back on that visit, I realize now the old woman must have been one of the Gods in disguise. I also realize they must have been controlling my thoughts to prevent me from questioning who she was.

In the morning, the old woman offered to help with some household chores to pay for our hospitality. I tried to refuse, but she insisted, and immediately went to the storeroom where the black chest was.

She hummed softly as she moved around the room straightening and organizing the collection of miscellaneous items accumulated over the years. She paused when she came to the chest. "This is very beautiful. What is in it?"

"Nothing," I said quickly. I moved to stand next to the chest, my hand resting on the lid. Without thinking, my fingers began to trace the delicately inlayed symbols.

The old woman reached out and took my hand in a grip that was cold and strong. I looked at her and found myself falling into her eyes: Eyes as black as the obsidian table in which I had first seen my reflection. However, nothing reflected in her eyes, they were deep and bottomless, reminders of the ancient night from which the first Gods were spawned.

I felt myself moving, but I had no control over my actions. She was guiding my hand across the chest and down to the clasp. My fingers seemed to move of their own accord and I watched as I removed the chain that held the clasp shut. A shock went through me and I was able to pull my hand away from the old woman. She smiled softly then vanished in a bright light. Despite the smile, I remember her eyes were sad.

For many minutes, I sat and stared at the black chest, trying to remember something. There was a fog in my mind and I couldn't seem to penetrate it. Shaking my head, I got up and left the storeroom, shutting the door behind me.

During the following days and weeks, I found myself drawn to the door of the storeroom every day, my hand reaching for the handle. Each time I stopped myself and moved on to other duties. This went on for many months, until another woman came asking for shelter. Again, I welcomed her into my home and provided food and a place to rest. Again, she insisted on performing some household chores to repay my kindness.

Just like the last traveler, she made her way to the storeroom where the chest was. This time, the old woman didn't make any pretense of working. She took my hand and guided me to the chest, pulling me down to my knees as my hand was guided to the clasp. No shock this time as I touched the gold clasp and lifted it slowly. The woman let go of my hand and patted my shoulder before she vanished.

I'm not sure how long I sat there staring at the chest, before I finally got up and left. This time, I hesitated before pulling the door shut.

For many weeks, I managed to put the incident out of my mind and didn't find myself drawn to the door of the storeroom. That is, until an old man came requesting shelter during the night. Again, hospitality was extended and accepted.

In the morning, when the old man left, he stopped at the door, took both my hands in his, and lifted them to his lips. "You have been a gracious hostess. May the Gods bless this house and those in it for many years," he said. For just a moment, his body seemed to fill out and he stood there straight, tall and powerful. His ancient eyes cleared and for a moment were the bright blue of the morning sky. "You are the gift of all and what you brought to

Man is very precious indeed. They are *all* gifts from the Gods." Without another word he turned and walked away, his carriage again frail and stooped with age.

I stood and watched until our visitor vanished from sight, then slowly closed the door. As I passed the storeroom, I heard his voice in my mind again. "They are *all* gifts from the Gods." I did not hesitate as I entered the room and knelt in front chest. With care, I lifted the lid.

As I looked in, I saw nothing except a deep blackness that fell away into nothing. A blackness that rivaled the darkest night when the moon is not visible in the sky. A blackness that perhaps would rival that of the pits of Tartarus itself. Slowly, something began moving in that blackness. A gray fog, that shimmered and moved as if alive. Was this the way the first Gods had been born out of the swirling mass that was the chaos from which they sprang?

The fog began flowing out of the chest: A rolling, swirling cloud of gray that quickly filled the room. As it touched and surrounded me, my skin tingled then burned then chilled. My lungs alternated between freezing and burning as I breathed the thickening air. Suddenly a sharp pain grabbed my joints and I fell to the floor. I watched as the skin on my hands and arms dried and shriveled. As quickly as the sensations came, they left. I raised my head slowly and saw a golden glow coming from the chest. As it seeped slowly out of the chest, warmth began filling the room and the gray cloud dissipated.

After the glow faded from the room, I looked in the chest and saw the endless black depths were now gone; all that was left was small shimmering, golden statue. I reached in and removed the small figure. As I studied it, it changed shape several times. First being a unicorn, then a small bird, then a beautiful woman with large wings, and many other shapes and beings. I placed the statue back in the chest and carefully secured the lid. Something told me this was the most precious thing that had been in the chest. "Elpis," I said softly. *Hope.*

It did not take long for the effects of opening the chest to become evident. The Golden Age was over. Disease and other problems began to plague Man. But, despite the despair that sometimes grew black and heavy, Hope was always there to lift Man up and support him through the darkest times.

~ * ~

By manipulating and controlling me, Zeus had his revenge on Prometheus for stealing fire and giving it to Man as well as for embarrassing him by tricking him into allowing Man to keep the best parts of the sacrifice. However, in the end, he still could not destroy Prometheus' creation. Instead, he made Man stronger and gave him Hope. Besides, what reason would Man have to worship the Gods, to ask for their help and make sacrifices if he never faced troubles and sorrows? None, and Zeus knew that. He also knew if Man ever realized that and they stopped worshipping the Gods, the Gods would cease to exist.

Legends blame me, in whichever guise you prefer, as being the cause of Man's troubles. I will admit I did open the chest, however, I was only a pawn in the game. The real blame still rests with the God, Goddess or Gods, depending on your religious views, who created the *gifts* then made sure they would be opened.

After all, most of them claim to be all knowing, and yet they created something they *claim* they did not want their creation to have then left it unguarded until it was taken or opened by that same creation. They then blame their creation for not following the rules they set down. If they *really* did not want us to have the knowledge or did not want to give us hardships to rise above, why did they create the knowledge or hardships in the first place? Something to think about, is it not?

As for me, I still have the chest and I still open it on occasion. Whenever things look dark and despair feels like it is crushing your soul, look for a woman with long black hair and sad, blue eyes, wearing a flowing blue Grecian gown and carrying a black chest. Just when you think hope is gone, I will open my box and let hope loose to fill your soul with new possibilities and ideas you may have missed. The greatest gift of the Gods will always be in my care, and I will never hesitate to pass it on to my children.

Adrift

Adrift.

Dewi couldn't believe she was actually adrift. Particularly not in space and not while *De Nederlander's* fuel cells were showing almost full. She knew there were members of the fleet as well as independent spacers who had nicknamed this area of the system the Sargasso Sea and others who compared it to the Bermuda Triangle. Both were references to old Earth legends. The Sargasso Sea—where the winds would stop blowing and the sea would be as still and smooth as polished glass; a place where a ship could be left stranded until her crew had perished from starvation and exposure. The Bermuda Triangle—where ships simply vanished and no traces could ever be found. Both places said to be cursed, just as some spacers where claiming this area was.

She glanced again at the power readings on her console. Internal power was still good, so she and her passenger didn't have to worry about starvation or exposure. Air shouldn't be a problem either. She leaned back in her chair and looked out at the empty space in front of her. She only had one choice now; let the ship drift until she was picked up or until *De Nederlander* was out of this area and able to travel under her own power again.

Normally she wouldn't have taken this route, legends about curses, or not, there *was* something about this area of the system that caused a ship's engines to shut down and no one had figured out what it was. However, her passenger had insisted on taking this specific route and had paid her extra for doing so.

Dewi glanced again at the positioning scanner. "Wait a minute," she said. "This can't be correct." She called up the chart showing her planned route, they matched. "We shouldn't be in the Sargasso yet," she said. "What's going on?"

Everything matched the few stories of ships that had lost power and been rescued, but *De Nederlander* was still several hours from where she expected to skirt the edge of the Sargasso Sea.

She hesitated as she reached for the emergency beacon. The

last reports she had seen indicated a group of pirates had taken up residence in this area of the system. If those reports were as accurate as the updated charts, then she had nothing to worry about. She shook her head to clear it. "Pirates." She laughed as she activated the beacon.

Dewi stood and stretched. All of the controls were locked and there was nothing she could do for now. The computer would alert her if someone responded to the emergency beacon. For now, all she could do was wait and make sure her passenger was okay. She paused and looked up at the sword hanging over the doorway. Her grandfather had given it to her for luck when she first started her courier service. He claimed the sword had been in their family for generations—going back to Earth and had once belonged to some long dead ancestor who had been captain of a ship lost at sea. The way her grandfather told the story, the sword had mysteriously arrived in the post, with no information on how or from where it had been sent, a few years after the ship had been declared lost. Since then, everyone in her family who captained a sailing vessel had carried the sword. No one else had been lost so the sword had come to be a symbol of luck for the Fokke family.

Her father had not wanted her to have the sword, because she had broken from tradition and decided to pilot a small space vessel instead of taking over his ship and continuing the family business on Nieuw Amsterdam. To tell the truth, she had been surprised he didn't disown her for abandoning the sea, but she was his only child and he could never stay mad at her for long.

She shook her head, she didn't believe in luck, any more than she believed it was some mystical curse that affected this area of the system. *Curses, legends and pirates,* she thought. *At least there is some humor to be found in the situation.* She shook her head as she walked down the corridor to the passenger cabins.

De Nederlander was a small transport ship, the latest in a long line of ships, though the first one that traveled through space and not on the sea, to bear the name—all of which had been in her family; at least all of the ones she knew about.

"Captain Fokke."

Dewi turned to see her passenger standing in the corridor.

"Mister Van der Decken." She studied the man standing in

47

front of her. His anachronistic style of dress had intrigued her when he had originally booked passage with her. The glossy black boots with the wide cuffs. The black pants stuffed into the boots and the white shirt with the billowing sleeves. Then to top everything off—the battered three-corner hat. She smiled and nodded.

"I take it we have entered the area known as the Sargasso Sea?" He leaned against the wall.

"We shouldn't be there yet," she said. She paused. "How did you...?"

"The engines have quieted and the feel of the deck is different."

"True." Unusual his appearance might be, but he was a true spacer. "You're the one who insisted on this route, I assume there is a reason?" She paused and waited.

"Curiosity can be a dangerous thing, Captain," he said. "After all curiosity killed the cat." He started to move past her.

"Mister Van der Decken, I do not like riddles or evasive answers to straightforward questions. You are the one who insisted we travel this route, even after I explained the reasons to not do so. If my ship has been put into danger because of your curiosity, I assure you—you will be the cat." She let her hand rest on the grip of her energy pistol.

"Ah, Captain." He raised his hands slightly. "Go ahead and shoot me with that toy. You will find that, like the engines, it is not functioning. This is a place where legends exist. You will need to be willing to face them on their terms in order to survive this voyage."

The ship rocked and Dewi grabbed for the wall as the sound of an explosion echoed in the corridor. Something sharp hit her neck and she spun around.

"Van der Decken!"

Smoke surrounded her and she lost sight of her passenger. She drew her pistol and made her way through the gray haze back to the control cabin. Before the door closed, she raised the pistol and squeezed the trigger—nothing. Van der Decken had been correct, the energy pistol wasn't working.

"In order to survive this voyage," she said as she slapped the door lock. "He knew what was going to happen." She dropped into the pilot's chair and checked the various monitors. Still, where they were when they had stopped. The emergency beacon was still transmitting, but there had been no notifications from the computer of another ship in the area. The external monitor clicked through all of the scanners—there were no other ships in the area. "What in the name of *Saeftinghe* is going on here?"

~ * ~

Dewi jumped as a shrill chirp sounded in the control cabin. She shook her head and glanced at the clock. Three hours had passed from the time *De Nederlander's* engines had stopped. She had fallen asleep—how could she have let that happen! Her ship was disabled and even if she didn't trust him, she was still responsible for her passenger's safety. The chirping continued. *Damn it, which alarm is it?* Her gaze darted over the control panel even as her hand went to the useless energy pistol. There—the airlock to the small cargo bay was being opened. She slapped the monitor controls until the scanner outside the cargo bay came up.

A small ship was attached to *De Nederlander* by a set of magnetic grapples and a transfer tether. *Pirates!* The reports were correct. Her hand tightened on the energy pistol then relaxed. She knew it wouldn't work in this area. She had already tested it. If her weapons and ship had lost power, how did the pirates manage to reach her? She focused the scanner on the ship; a large solar sail shimmered against the darkness. The material appeared to glow and she could see the symbol painted on it: a rampant lion holding a sword in his right paw and skull in his left. Around the lion was a wreath of leaves and oranges.

"What are they after?" She wasn't carrying any cargo, she never did. All she ever carried were passengers from one of the various terra-formed worlds in this system to another. "Van der Decken!" She grabbed the sword from the wall and headed for the passenger quarters.

Two men, also armed with swords met her in the corridor. She kept her sword in a low guard position, thankful her grandfather and father had both insisted she learn the archaic weapon style. The smiles on the faces of her opponents told her they didn't think much of the way she was holding the weapon—which was what she wanted them to think. Still, there were two of them and she only had one sword—she was at a distinct disadvantage if they were smart enough to attack together. She frowned as the two men moved toward her. They were smart enough.

She shifted the blade a bit, then realized she was still holding the scabbard in the other hand. She could use it to block with if she needed to. She smiled as the two men hesitated when she brought the scabbard up and repositioned the sword. *I can't afford to play games,* she thought. She turned slightly, moving so she would able to get her back to the wall.

"Hold!"

Dewi continued to watch the two men, her sword held in front of her.

"Hold!" The command came again.

The two men stepped back, but never took their eyes off her. She glanced to the side see Van der Decken. He stood with two more men, each dressed as unusually as he was and also holding swords.

"What is this all about?"

"You."

"Me?" Dewi took a step back then stopped as her back met the wall.

Van der Decken took a step forward. "You and that sword you're carrying." He held his hand out.

Dewi pulled the sword closer to her. "This sword has been in my family for centuries. You don't think I'm going to just give it to you."

"Of course not. But, I imagine you would be willing to give it back to the original owner."

"The original owner?" Dewi stared at him. "As I said, this sword has been in my family for centuries. I doubt Captain Bernard Fokke is going to be showing up to claim it anytime soon."

Van der Decken laughed as he held his hand out. "Bernard was not the original owner of that sword. Now hand it over."

"I think not." She brought sword back into a guard position. "You'll have to take it."

"You are a fool, just as Bernard was. Just as I was. So be it." He nodded.

Dewi fell back against the wall as something stabbed into her neck. She blinked several times as everything began shifting and spinning. The last thing she remembered was hearing the sound of the sword echoing in her ears as it hit the deck and blackness surrounded her.

~ * ~

Dewi woke slowly, the pounding in her heart matching the beat of her heart, as they each seemed to be trying to outdo each other for volume. She was still surrounded by darkness and the tingling of energy around her wrists told her she was now a prisoner of these pirates. *Legends, curses and pirates,* she thought. Obviously, the reports about pirates were more accurate than she had thought they were. *So if those reports were correct, what does that mean about the legends and curses?* She wasn't sure she wanted to know.

She thought about her family's history as she continued to sit in the dark. Van der Decken probably didn't think she knew much about the legends associated with her ancestor Bernard or with a distant namesake of his—Captain Hendrik Van der Decken. Both where credited in different legends with being the Captain of the "Flying Dutchman". Of course, there was also that silly twenty-first century story about Davy Jones being the Captain of the "Dutchman" as well. Three different legends and three different curses. How did she or Bernard's sword tie into any of them? There was something telling her all of this was connected. It couldn't just be a coincidence she was carrying a passenger with the last name of Van der Decken. And that same passenger apparently knew these pirates and was interested in Bernard's sword.

Dewi blinked as the lights came on in the room. The polished walls created dancing stars in front of her and she closed her eyes again to stop the throbbing she felt in her head.

"Bring her." Van der Decken's voice echoed in the small room.

Dewi didn't struggle as she felt someone grab each of her arms and pull her to her feet. She waited until the brightness she saw through her eyelids, faded then opened them slowly.

"Welcome to *De Vliegende Hollander* Captain Fokke," Van der Decken said bowing.

De Vliegende Hollander? The Flying Dutchman? What is going on here? Dewi looked around. The portholes showed the empty area of space they were in, but the deck was covered in wood, as were the walls. Ropes and hooks hung on the walls lending to the feel the ship was designed to look like a sea going vessel instead of a space vessel. "Mister Van der Decken, perhaps you should do more research—*De Vliegende Hollander* was not the name of Captain Fokke's vessel. That nickname was earned because of the speed of his vessel."

"Speed that was gained after he made a deal with supernatural forces."

She smiled. "Of course. He deserves no credit for being able to read the winds or sea or for his part in helping to design the keel of his ship. That his was one of the fastest ships to sail the seas at that time had to be because of a deal with the devil."

Van der Decken shook his head then motioned for one of the other to remove the energy restraints on her wrists. She rubbed them a couple of times as the tingle faded.

"It wasn't a deal with the devil, but with Nehalennia."

"Nehalennia? The protector of sea travelers. Her worship died out centuries before the legends of *The Dutchman* began."

"True, but she was patient deity who understood the cyclic nature of the gods and the fickleness of humans." He gestured to a pair of leather-covered chairs. "Please sit and I'll explain."

Dewi leaned back in the chair, but refused to relax as at least two of Van der Decken's men stood on either side of her.

"Why should I trust what you tell me?" She asked. "You disabled my ship somehow, then illegally boarded her and kidnapped me. Just because there is a lot of romanticism about pirates—doesn't mean you can get away with this."

"Nor does it mean we are trustworthy, pirate's code or no pirate's code."

This time Dewi smiled and nodded.

"You can judge for yourself after you hear my story."

She gestured for him to proceed.

"Bernard was one of the best sailors and part of that was because he understood and respected the sea. Something most Hollanders do. Even in this new world our ties to the sea are still strong."

Dewi cleared her throat.

"Did you know the root of your name, Dewi, was a Celtic sea god—some people believe he was the origin of the legends of Davy Jones?"

"And this has what to do with why you've kidnapped me and stolen Captain Bernard's sword?" She leaned forward a bit and felt a hand on her shoulder stopping her from standing.

"Not much at this stage of the tale. As I was saying he was a great sailor. Something he did though was pay his respects at the shrines of all the sea gods and goddesses and never restricted his men from honoring those they chose to honor. While a Christian himself, he also said it didn't hurt to remember all the names of God and who was to say which one He favored that particular day. It was for this reason he chose an image of Nehalennia as the figurehead of his ship. And she, appreciating his tolerance of others and his respect for the elder ways and the sea granted his vessel its legendary speed."

He paused and looked at her, his head cocked to the side. "What stories does your family tell to explain how his sword came back to them when the reports said all hands were lost?"

"It was always assumed there had to have been at least one survivor, one who just didn't want to be known as the sole survivor of Captain Fokke's last voyage. After the legends of The Flying Dutchman began to appear, it became even more likely he didn't want anyone to know about him."

"Ah, so you do know the other legends."

"Of course I do, and I even know how your family name ties into them as well."

"Well the legends are not always the truth. Hendrik was never the captain of that ill-fated vessel. However, he was the cause of them being damned as they were."

"So you're kidnapping me is just something you had to do to carry on the family tradition—so to speak."

"No." Even though his voice was still smooth and even, she could read the anger in his eyes and in the way his hands clenched against the arms of the chair.

He sat silently for several seconds but she refused to drop her gaze from his face. He finally nodded and continued.

"When one walks with the gods as closely as Bernard did, they will sometimes test them. Think of Job from the Old Testament. Hendrik was Bernard's test. He was indeed a pirate and he had attempted to take Bernard's ship. He was defeated and gave over his sword to Captain Fokke in exchange for his life. He was allowed to stay on the ship, as Bernard didn't want to release him back to begin pirating again, but he wasn't grateful for the chance he was given. He hid a secret from his captain and crewmates. He was carrying a plague that began to affect them. It was during that final trip around the Cape that the crew was stricken."

He paused and looked down at his hands.

Dewi waited—her initial anger gone. Now she understood. He wasn't here to kidnap or steal her ship, he was looking to lay the ghosts of his past to rest by facing her, the last descendant of Bernard Fokke.

"They were to have put in at Table Bay," she said softly.

"Aye, that they were, but with the crew sick as they were, Bernard tried to put in at Duikerpunt, but the harbormaster refused them entry. Wouldn't take a chance on the plague spreading through the port. Bernard understood his reasoning and turned back to his original course. They were assailed by a strong wind as a storm swept down on them and it was after night had fallen they reached their destination."

Hendrik argued they should pull down the plague flag Bernard was flying and make port before anyone knew there was a problem on board, but Bernard denied this request. Some say even the figurehead of Nehalennia told him they should put in under the cover of nightfall. The legends say Bernard cursed all of the gods he had ever honored for bringing the pestilence to his ship and swore he would beat about the oceans until the Day of Judgment before he would risk bringing the disease to Cape Town.

"So unlike Job he failed when he was tested," he said.

"Did he? Yes, he cursed the gods and bound himself to sail the seas eternally, but he didn't condemn others to death as would have happened. Surely the gods understood that."

"Perhaps." He gestured and one of the men placed her sword on her lap. "And truthfully, he has accepted his fate as he spoke it—though he mourns for his crew and has searched for a way to save them from this eternal damnation."

"Okay, what does all this have to do with me?"

"We've have come to you to release us."

"Us?"

Her hands tightened on the scabbard.

Van der Decken stood and bowed slightly. "Hendrik van der Decken at your service, Captain Fokke. When Bernard accepted by oath to serve his ship, I gave him that sword as my pledge to serve faithfully. While I was argumentative and often questioned the way he did things, I did serve faithfully. By releasing me from that service, you can release all of us."

"And what will happen to you then? From what you said, Bernard refused to release you from his ship for fear you return to pirating. Now, it looks like you have done so anyway." She stood and jerked away from the guard who had his hand on her shoulder and moved to look out the porthole. "I see no sign of a sea vessel only my small transport. If you are indeed the same Hendrik Van der Decken who sailed with Bernard Fokke, how is it we are not on *The Flying Dutchman* or the oceans of Earth?"

She turned back to face him.

"Because the sword is no longer on Earth, or on a sea going vessel. Check the records, you will find the reports of pirates started shortly after you launched *De Nederlander*."

"Yet, the reports of something that robs ships of their power in this area have been around far longer." She pulled the sword part way from the scabbard and looked down at the image etched in the metal near the hand guard. A lion rampant; holding a sword in his upraised paw, with a wreath of oranges and leaves surrounding him. Missing was the skull that appeared in the lion's other hand on the solar sail.

"That I have no answer to." He paused and grinned. "Although, we have made use of those reports—as you have seen."

"Captain Fokke, enough of this. Will you release us from the oaths binding us to *The Flying Dutchman* and allow us to finally find peace?

She stepped back, drew the sword and held it before her. Then in one swift motion, she spun the blade and held it out, the hilt toward Van der Decken. "Your service has been noted and you are free to seek your own path. However, I would charge you with no longer following the life of a pirate. However, while I do not lay this charge on you I hope you will honor it."

He placed his hand on the sword and nodded. "I will honor your request. I have had enough of wandering aimlessly; whether it be through life or undeath. I will pass into legend and finally find peace—as will the crew. The sword I give to you, a gift so you will remember us."

She sheathed the sword, nodded and smiled. She waited, as he seemed to grow paler and paler until it seemed only an apparition stood before her. She turned to see the other two had also faded.

She sheathed the sword and slipped it into her belt as another person stepped into the room. A tall man with shoulder length, sun streaked brown hair; dressed in the same fashion as the others.

"Come Dewi, I will escort you back to your vessel and then I will take these souls to a place where they will find peace." He gestured to the doorway.

"Bernard Fokke?" She asked as they walked down the corridor.

"I would say at your service, but I have another service I am bound to."

"Your crew."

"My crew. One of the oaths, I gave to Nehalennia was that I always see to the safety of my crew. I failed in that oath, when I placed the safety of Cape Town above theirs and refused to make port. With the plague flag flying, we were continually denied the right to make port at any we came to until all finally succumbed to the disease except me. She has granted me the chance to redeem myself and I will honor it." He opened the airlock and nodded toward the tether still stretched between the two ships. "Fair winds to you Captain Fokke."

She held out the sword.

He held up his hands. "No, it is yours."

"Fair winds, Captain Fokke," she said.

~ * ~

Dewi watched as the grapples and tether disconnected from her ship then turned her attention to the small vessel as it turned to head deeper into the area known as the Sargasso Sea. As she watched, another image overlaid itself on the ship. "Fair winds," she whispered as the image of a Dutch sailing vessel of the seventeenth century faded into the darkness.

The Second Horseman

Sunlight streamed through the large stained glass windows lining the walls of the sanctuary. They were positioned so the light would fall on the large dais and pulpit; almost like spotlights controlled by heaven. Reverend James Smallman glanced up at the center window on the back wall and smiled as the warmth of the light fell on his face. The glass showing Moses' and his staff destroying the staves of the Pharaoh's magicians and proving the power of the one true God was his favorite scene.

"My Brothers and Sisters," he said as he stepped around the pulpit, and looked out at the sanctuary. The Lord had certainly blessed his work during the last few years; today's overflow congregation was proof of that. *And, why wouldn't He?* James thought. *I speak the truth, direct from Him.*

"I had prepared a sermon of Thanksgiving on this, the tenth anniversary of our ministry. However, something happened to change that." James paused, walked the length of the dais making eye contact with many in the congregation and the broadcast cameras.

"You may ask what is so important it would cause me to forego my planned sermon." James stepped back around the pulpit, picked up a book and raised it above his head. "This is a textbook that my daughter, Diana, brought home from school last week. The title of this book is 'Gods of the Ancient and Modern World.'

"This morning, Diana told me her teacher was telling her students the people of the ancient world were not condemned for their faith in false gods, but would be judged based on their beliefs."

Collective gasp sounded from the congregation and James smiled and nodded.

"Once again the world chooses to attack us and the Living God. It began with evolution; teaching our children that man was not created by divine hands, but evolved from a monkey." James paused as shouts of "Amen" resounded through the sanctuary.

"Now, they presume to teach that false gods are real!" He slammed the book down on the pulpit. "We must take a stand! We must not allow this blasphemy to continue!" James gestured and two men wheeled a large barrel out in front of the pulpit.

One of the men tossed a match into the barrel, igniting the fuel inside. James picked up the textbook, and brandished it over his head. "Just as the flames in this barrel will cleanse and purify the blasphemy in this book, we must cleanse and purify those who don't believe in the Living God. Let the cleansing begin!" James hurled the book into the barrel.

"You are summoned, James Smallman, to account for your actions," a powerful voice, which was neither male nor female, yet seemed to be both, called. The sanctuary vibrated with the power in that voice.

James looked up and saw a tall, light-haired woman, dressed in silver garments stepping to the edge of the upper balcony edge. She stood in front of the window showing Moses and the staves. The light surrounded her, creating a bright aura that burned and shimmered. A silver bow was in her hands, aimed at his heart. He heard a creak and a rush of air then felt the silver arrow strike his chest. The sanctuary vanished in a flash of light.

When the light faded, James found himself standing by a lake shrouded in mist. "What is this? Where am I?" he demanded.

"This is the afterlife, James Smallman," said the same voice he had heard in the sanctuary. "One version of it. It changes dependent on the faith and beliefs of those who come."

"This is not part of my beliefs. I deny this place, I deny you!"

Another flash of light and James found himself standing on a hill looking at three crosses. "I never denied you," the figure on the middle cross, said softly.

"This is a trick! I deny all of this!" James cried. This time the scene dissolved into a gray expanse of nothingness.

A figure stepped out of the shadows. "This is where your faith has brought you, James Smallman. Or, perhaps more appropriately, your lack of faith."

James stared at the figure, which remained shrouded in gray.

"My faith? That cannot be—this does not match anything I know about Heaven."

"Therein lies your problem, James Smallman. That which you have learned is not necessarily the same as that which you believe. To learn something is not the same as accepting it on faith. This place reflects your lack of true faith."

"No! That cannot be! I know in what I believe!"

"Then prove it. Demonstrate your faith and bring yourself to the place you believe reserved for you."

When the figure finished speaking, James found himself surrounded by a multitude of unidentifiable figures. "Who you are and why have you brought me here?" he asked.

"We are those who have been worshiped throughout time as gods, guardian spirits, angels and a host of other names. You have been brought here as a result of your own actions. Are you prepared to be judged?" the voice asked.

"Yes! I know I am ready to face judgment."

"Very well. The assemblage is called!"

The gray mists parted to reveal a great stadium filled with thousands of spectators. James stood in front of a table on which sat an ebony scale. Next to the scale stood two manlike figures: one with the head of a jackal, the other a bird. "Who are you to sit in judgment over me? I do not believe in you!" James said.

"That will not work here, James Smallman," the voice said.

"You must show us what you believe in, not what you don't. If you fail to do so, you will be judged by these assembled."

"I am a child of The Lamb. I will only be judged by Him!"

"Finally, you call on me. Yes, you are one of mine, James, and I claim you as such." A figure walked up, dressed in simple robes and sandals. On the side of his dusty robes and in his outstretched palms, James saw blood.

"My Lord!" James fell to his knees.

"Rise, my child." Christ reached down and lifted James to his feet.

"Lord, what is this place? I do not understand what has been happening."

"It is enough for you to know I am with you. I ask you, James, do you truly wish to see the world cleansed in the manner in which you spoke?" Christ asked.

"Yes!"

The voice spoke again. "And when the second seal was broken, there went out a red horse: and power was given unto him that sat thereon to take peace from the Earth, and that they should kill one another: and there was given unto him a great sword."

"Revelations six: four," James said.

"You are correct. The Book of Revelations is one of many prophecies about the end of the world. That time is here, and you, James Smallman, will be allowed to play an important part in the events to come," the voice said.

"And, what part would that be?" James demanded.

Christ smiled sadly. "You haven't guessed yet?" he asked.

"You are to be the catalyst which will trigger the coming of the Second Horseman. The first has been riding across Earth for decades. It is now time for the second."

A mirror appeared and began to reflect dozens of images. Images of war. James watched as the Christian banner was carried into battle, and he saw thousands dying in the names of their chosen Gods.

The images changed, and James saw his death. Instead of the woman with the bow, this time a man, dressed in dusty robes and wearing a dirty turban burst into the church carrying a gun. "Jihad!" The man's voices echoed in the large room and he brought the gun up to his shoulder and pulled the trigger, spraying automatic gunfire around the sanctuary. "For Allah. The infidels must die."

James cringed as he saw the bullets strike him and he fell to the floor. Suddenly, a beam of white light pierced the ceiling and the gunman was struck, leaving only a pile of smoking ashes. He watched as his body was lifted up by another, softer light and carried out of the church. The sanctuary was filled with a golden radiance and a powerful voice repeated his last words to the kneeling congregation. "Let the cleansing begin!"

The scene in the mirror shifted again, this time James found himself watching as a large group gathered in St. Peter's Square.

"We have been witness to a great miracle," the Pope said to the crowd. "One of the Lord's Chosen was taken to Heaven by the hand of God itself. Before his ascension, Reverend James Smallman spoke of the way the world has been trying to destroy God. He called for all of Christianity to unite and cleanse our world. As he was taken, the voice of God spoke, reiterating the words of James Smallman.

"We have been given a sign and a message: Let the cleansing begin!" The mirror went dark.

"Many of your prophecies speak of the world being destroyed in fire and so it shall. The coming of the Second Horseman will open the third and fourth seals. One Horseman following the other," the voice declared.

"This is not what I envisioned. Who are you that you cause this tragedy?" James demanded.

"I am that I am. I am neither God nor Goddess. I am all that is, all that shall be. Christ, you may escort James Smallman to the place which has been prepared for him."

"You still haven't told me why!"

"Why was the Earth destroyed by a flood?" The voice softened. "Because it was necessary."

"James, come with me. In my father's house are many mansions. I have prepared a place for you." Christ led him down a street paved with gold.

The President's Meow

It's hard to say when the changed actually happened. Other than his wife and children, I am probably closer to the President than anyone else is. Before I go any further, I should probably introduce myself. Then again, maybe I shouldn't. Let's just say I have been with the President since his political career began. I have worked with and advised him through good times and bad. If you really need something to call me, let's make it Michael.

In all the years I have known the President, he has always been a bit peculiar. In recent years, he has had to deal with personal issues and the scandals that have occurred during his time in the White House. Then again, name a President who hasn't had to deal with those to one extent or another. Americans love scandal and gossip, and they seem to expect it from their political leaders. Still behind the closed doors of the Oval Office, he was an intelligent and capable leader. You didn't necessarily have to agree with his political views to agree with that.

The first time I noticed something unusual was the day the Heads of State, and their entourages, arrived from several Middle Eastern countries for a series of meetings with the President and other Western leaders. Introductions went smoothly enough, although I saw a slight scrunching of the President's face as he shook hands with the members of the Egyptian delegation. I couldn't help thinking when I saw this expression, that if he had whiskers he would have been putting them forward. Fortunately, our guests didn't seem to notice or at least they didn't take offense at the gesture. He finished his prepared greeting, glanced at me then turned his back and left.

There were a few raised eyebrows at this, but no one commented on his behavior. Of course, they may have assumed other matters were distracting him. As I handed out the information and welcome packets then introduced the VIP's to their Secret Service escorts, I noticed the Egyptian Ambassador's aide, an elaborately gowned and jeweled woman, almost reminiscent of ancient Egypt, was smiling softly as she followed the President's departure with her bright blue eyes.

The next obvious incident came the next day, following a meeting with his advisors and various members of the delegations to work out the final schedule for the meetings. He insisted on sitting in on the meeting and had invited the other Heads of State to do the same. I wasn't at the meeting, having to handle several points of protocol with the Egyptian Ambassador. Thankfully, nothing like what I saw went on during the meeting; or least not that I ever heard. With the number of people in the meeting, someone would have said something if anything had happened.

I was gathering the papers and notes left behind in the room, when I heard what sounded like purring coming from behind one of the larger chairs. I briefly thought about calling one of the Secret Service agents in from the corridor, but rejected that idea. After all, it was probably only one of the White House cats—right? Wrong! It was the President.

Lying in a patch of sunlight behind the brown leather chair, the President of the United States was playing with a piece of thread hanging from the bottom of the chair.

I shook my head as I watched him batting at the thread. What would cause him to act like this? I knew he was under a lot of stress recently, with the meeting and the press blowing the latest scandal out of proportion, as usual, as well as his upcoming State of the Union Address. However, this...this made no sense. This was also an election year. News of his strange behavior could not be allowed to get past these doors. There's an old saying: Three people can keep a secret, but only if two are dead. No place is that more true than in Washington where gossip and scandal are the stock in trade of so many. If I didn't want any of this to get out to the media, I would have to deal with it myself.

I stepped back over to the desk and coughed loudly. After a moment, he stood up from behind the chair and smoothed his suit jacket.

"I didn't hear you come in," he said holding something in his hand.

I nodded politely. "My apologies, if I disturbed you. Should I come back later to take care of these papers?"

"No, go ahead. I was just looking for my pin." He held up a

small cat-shaped lapel pin. The brushed silver figure seemed to stare at me with eyes the same color as the Ambassador's aide. He dropped the pin into his pocket and headed for the door then paused for a moment. "Make sure I get a copy of the compiled notes as soon as they're ready," he said.

"Yes, Sir." I turned my attention back to gathering the papers. On a small scrap of paper, someone had doodled a sketch of a cat pouncing on a small mouse. I glanced at the doors behind me then placed the sketch in my pocket. Was this the work of someone bored during the meeting who liked cats? Or, did it indicate how someone in the meeting or someone they were working for felt about the President's dealings with the Middle East? Recent events in the Middle East made these talks precarious, they could help stabilize the situation or tip the scales toward a war that would sweep across the region. Many felt the United States was trying to manipulate events so they could have a stronger hold on the area and they had become vocal in their resentment.

~ * ~

I next noticed something strange a few afternoons later when I brought his dog by for their daily walk. The VIP's had been taken on a private tour of several museums and he had taken advantage of the break to work on his upcoming State of the Union Address. He had spent all morning on the speech, without even taking a break for lunch. I figured taking the dog for a walk would do him some good. Give him a break and he could return to the speech fresh.

As soon as we stepped through those large doors, I had to grab the leash with both hands to hold the stupid mutt. He was lunging at the desk, barking his fool head off. The President responded to this by jumping onto his desk and hissing. He was on his hands and knees, his back arched—just like an alley cat meeting a dog. He then slapped the dog across the face with his right hand.

The dog sat down suddenly and cocked his head at the President who climbed off the desk, smoothed his jacket and held his hand out for the leash as if nothing unusual had just happened. "Thanks for bringing him by. I need a break and the fresh air should help clear my mind," the President said as I handed him the leash.

~ * ~

Later that night I was given more cause to worry. Being one of those aides who had to be available twenty-four/seven, I had rooms in the White House. After handling a few more complaints from the VIP's, I was able to crawl into bed around midnight. It was approximately two in the morning when I awakened to the sound of something howling. At least, I thought it was howling.

I pulled on a pair of pants and a shirt and went to investigate. Probably nothing more than a tomcat trying to serenade a queen, I thought as I exited the residential wing. I paused for a moment glancing around, and caught my breath as I thought about the connection I had made to cats again. Hoping it actually was a pair of felines involved in a mating ritual, I moved swiftly through the shadows following the sound.

Two members of the Secret Service blocked my path as I came around a corner of the building.

"Sorry, this area is off limits," the older of the two said in that professional monotone way they have of speaking. I always wondered if talking in a specific manner was one of the classes Secret Service agents had to take during their training.

"Is it him again?" I tried to sound like I knew what was going on, even though I was hoping I was wrong.

The second agent looked at me, and I was surprised to see the faint trace of a smile on his lips and in his eyes. "I'm sorry; Sir, but we can't discuss that."

Abruptly the noise stopped and the President walked over to join us. He had a slightly dazed looked on his face as his eyes darted from me to the two agents standing there. However, he didn't say anything, only pushed past us and back into the White House. I looked at the two agents and frowned. "You didn't see any of this," I said sharply. "If anyone asks about the noise, you chased off some stray cats. Got it!" I didn't wait for their answers, only hurried after the President. I wasn't worried about the senior agent; the fact the younger man had found the situation amusing bothered me. I would have to have a private discussion with him later, to make sure he understood his duty to the President and his country. Most agents could be counted on to keep things they saw or heard while dealing with the President and other officials secret. It was part of their training and something expected of them. If there were any chance they would be even a small risk they never made it through their training. However, they were only human and it seemed like leaks about activities within the White House had been increasing during the past few administrations. Granted nothing involving National Security had been put at risk unless you counted the declining respect other national leaders had for the United States and her political system.

"Mister President!" I hurried through the corridors trying to catch him before he made to his family's private residential area.

He stopped and turned to me, and I noticed a flash of silver and blue on his collar. It was the small cat figure.

"Yes, Michael?" His hand went to the pin and rubbed it a few times.

"Is anything wrong? Anything your staff should know about?"

"Nothing. Why?"

"If I may speak plainly?"

He nodded once and I continued. "You seem to be more distracted than usual these past few weeks. I understand you're concerned about these meetings, but I think something else is affecting you, Sir. After all, midnight strolls have not been on your schedule before."

"I'm sorry if that's your perception. However, the only thing bothering me is these talks. The problems facing the Middle East and U.S. interests in that region at this time are enormous and the interference of previous administrations hasn't helped the situation. We helped create the mess and we have an obligation to help clean it up. Nevertheless, we must tread very carefully, because we could make it that much worse as well. I'm not sure I'm up to the challenge."

"I have complete confidence in your abilities to handle this, Sir. You shouldn't worry so much."

His hand moved to the cat pin and touched it lightly. "That makes one of you."

"Despite the rumors and stories in the press, Sir, there are a lot more people than just me who still believe in you."

He smiled—an increasingly rare expression these days.

"Thank you." He started to leave.

"If I may ask, where did you get the pin from?"

He stopped and looked at me; his head cocked to the side.

I pointed to the silver cat pin.

"Oh, this. The Egyptian Ambassador's aide gave it to me. She said it would bring me luck. Apparently, cats were once highly revered by some Middle Eastern cultures. The Egyptians deified them—messengers of the Gods or something like that. They even worshipped the cat goddess Bast."

"Then may it bring you luck."

"Thank you." He turned abruptly and walked away.

As I watched him, my mind was still on the cat-shaped pin. It made no sense for the Ambassador's aide to give him a personal gift. It went against protocol and the fact it was presented by the aide and not through the proper channels made me suspicious. Why would she give it to him?

As I slowly walked back to my rooms, I realized I wasn't going to get any sleep that night.

~ * ~

I shut down my computer and glanced out at the brightening sky. The sun, The Eye of Ra, a title sometimes applied to the Cat-Goddess Bast. She who was also seen as the avenger of Ra. Despite the conflicting information in the various versions of her mythology, I was able to find; the role of render, tearer, and avenger was mentioned in most of them. It was this image that was bothering me the most. Why give the President a token that related to an ancient Egyptian Goddess for luck, when that Goddess wasn't associated with luck, but instead with vengeance.

Could the charm be what was affecting his recent behavior? If so, why would anyone want the President to begin behaving like a cat? To discredit him? Considering the image I had of Bast as avenger, could this be revenge motivated? Possibly—but who would be the most likely and why? Of course, the obvious answer was someone in the group from the Middle East. The Egyptian Ambassador's aide, and that pointed to either him or her as the most likely suspect, had given the charm to him. That it had been presented outside the normal protocols also added to my concern.

The question now became how to find out who was behind

this and how to protect the President. At least, protect him long enough to complete these talks. A cold shower and a hot pot of coffee would help to wake me up, I only hoped I could remain alert and close to the President throughout the day.

~ * ~

The first series of meetings went well. No tempers flaring, it wasn't until we broke for lunch that I noticed something happen. I was again picking up papers and changing the recording tapes when one of the interns walked in. The President had sat down in one of the overstuffed leather chairs, his eyes closed and head back as he relaxed for a few minutes, before joining his guests for lunch. His eyes opened quickly and followed the intern's movements closely as I gave her the tapes and notes to be organized and transcribed.

Without a word, the President got up and left the office. I was relieved to see he didn't follow the intern down the hallway. I finished straightening the office and headed for the dining room. I was at the doors, when a scream pierced the air. One of the agents at the door rushed into the room, while the other moved to prevent anyone else from entering. I was pacing the hallway when the doors slammed against the walls and the First Lady practically ran out of the room. The agents assigned to her were following closely behind.

The agent at the entrance was still recovering from being hit in the back of the head by one of the doors and I was able to slip into the dining room. The President stood with his back in the corner, with two other agents standing on either side of him. The Middle Eastern leaders, who had been in the dining hall, were all yelling at each other, occasionally pointing at the President, in their native languages. It was doubtful anyone could actually understand what was being shouted in the cacophony.

Near the delegates, I noticed one of the Secret Service agents—the same young man from the previous night. He looked at me and I saw a hint of a smile on his face as he nodded toward one of the plates. On the plate, in the middle of the salad lay a large rat, its head bent back, apparently broken.

"Get him out of here!" I pointed toward the President.

One of the agents touched the President's elbow, then

stepped back as he hissed and brought his hand up like a claw. I immediately stepped over and yanked the silver cat pin off the President's lapel. The cloth of his suit ripped loudly and he shook his head, his eyes clearing. I watched as they changed from cat-like slits back to the normal round pupil of a human eye. He didn't say anything as the Secret Service agents escorted him from the room.

"My apologies for the disruption, Gentlemen." I bowed slightly, my hands held out from my side as I addressed the VIP's. "If you will return to your rooms, we will have meals delivered to you shortly. With your consent we will continue our discussions tomorrow afternoon."

The dignitaries all nodded and began filing out the door with their escorts. As the young agent from last night passed, I grabbed his arm and pulled him toward me.

I tensed waiting for his reaction; surprisingly none came. He only looked at me and smiled. "Yes, Sir?"

"Come with me—we need to talk."

The young man followed me to one of the small conference rooms. "What can I do for you?" He carefully shut the door behind us.

"Agent Land, isn't it?"

He nodded, the smile never leaving his face.

"I'm concerned about your apparent amusement over the situation last night and just now."

"You needn't be. I am not going to pass anything to the press about this. However, you have to admit the cat behavior of last night and at lunch is amusing."

"No, Agent Land, I do not. If this was occurring during a time when nothing at all was happening; then it might, I repeat it *might* be amusing. As it is, it is not amusing in the slightest. I expect you to maintain a professional attitude at all times from here on out, or I will see to it you are reassigned."

"Understood, Sir." The smile vanished from his face. "Will that be all?"

I dropped into one of the chairs. "It is," I said as I leaned back and closed my eyes. There was a soft click as Agent Land closed the door behind him.

After a few minutes, I sat back up and stared at the door. Something had to be done to salvage this situation and fast. But what? I looked down at the pin, still in my hand. There had to be another trigger, other than just the pin. After all, he wasn't constantly acting like a cat while wearing the pin. I doubted it was location, since he wasn't in the Oval Office last night. I thought back on what I had observed prior to each of the incidents.

It was obvious the President was being influenced to act like a cat. Was there some common factor other than the pin? In the first meeting with the dignitaries, before he had received the pin, he had scrunched his face up, much like a cat putting its whiskers forward when greeting another creature, he had also finished with the formal greetings then turned his back and walked off. As someone who had lived around cats growing up, I knew they could be seen as anti-social for their tendency to leave when they were done with whatever they were doing. The next incident came when I found the President lounging in a patch of sunlight batting a piece of string. That same day I had found the piece of paper with the pouncing cat drawn on it. It was few days later, that he and his dog had their little confrontation. Unless someone had stopped by the Oval Office before I did, there would have been no other common persons present in all of those events, other than myself. I frowned, could I be the trigger somehow? Moreover, if I was, how? I didn't have any reason to wish ill toward the President.

Of course, the idea I might be an additional trigger didn't hold up when I considered the serenading of the previous night, as I had had no contact with him for several hours prior to that incident. Then what about today's incident? What I had taken as possible inappropriate attention to one of the female intern's might have been related to the presentation of the rat on the First Lady's salad.

Again, I could not place any common thread to these events that might possibly provide a trigger other than the pin. Perhaps, the pin was the only trigger and it was designed to work in an intermittent manner, resulting in occasional behavior changes. I had no way of actually knowing.

I looked down at the silver pin, its bright blue eyes sparkling in the light from my desk lamp. How did I break the magic of this talisman? I doubted disfiguring the pin would work; perhaps I could melt it down and release the magic that way.

Hoping I was right, I started a fire in the fireplace in my room. Here it was the middle of July and I had a fire going. Hopefully, no one would notice. I wrapped the pin in a ball of paper then tossed it into the middle of the flames. I continued to feed the fire as I watched the pin glow. Several minutes later the silver began softening and pooling in the bottom of the fireplace. The bright blue jewels, now black and dull floated down the silver stream. I reached in with the poker, shifted them out of the shining pool, and pulled them to the edge of the hearth to cool. Now, all I could do was wait and hope this was enough to disrupt the power of the charm. Picking up the still warm *eyes*, I placed them inside one the lock boxes in my desk.

~ * ~

The next day things seemed to be normal, well at least as normal as life in the White House could be. I observed no unusual behavior in the President as he went about his duties. Standing in front of my door that night, I finally released the wisp of breath I had been holding all day.

Opening the door, I saw a small black and white cat sitting on my desk. The delicate creature turned slowly and I found myself being silently appraised by a pair of brilliant blue eyes; the same color as the Egyptian Ambassador aide's eyes and the silver cat pin I had destroyed the night before.

I closed the door behind me then bowed my head respectfully toward the cat. "Lady Bast," I said.

The cat smiled, nodded and leaped off the table. Before the feline landed, she had changed into the aide. "I am surprised you recognize me," she said softly, a soft purr was in her voice as she spoke.

"Why?" I shuddered at the smile the Goddess gave me. Even with a human face, there was something feral and dangerous in that look.

"Because prey still deserve respect, and your leaders no longer respect those they view as prey. Perhaps, when you lose the respect of your prey and the other predators and even become prey yourselves you will understand. Despite the changes you have forced on others who are different from you, many still hold to the old ways and beliefs. They have called on me to help them now."

I could only stare at the Goddess. Her words had struck a chord of truth. However, they were not the whole truth. "Lady, I understand your concerns and those of your children. However, there are times when we must make decisions that affect others. Others have forced us into the role of mediator and protector. They look to us to intervene and assist. When we do, we are called arrogant and those that are unhappy with our decisions complain. When we do not, we are still called arrogant and everyone complains. Many mistakes have been made by our leaders; that I will not deny. However, we continue to learn from those mistakes. There was a time when your children were in the same position as leaders of the world during their time. Did they never cause the children of other Gods or Goddesses to complain? Did they never lose respect for their prey?"

I waited as the Goddess appeared to consider my words. Everyone made mistakes; I only hoped I hadn't made one in questioning Bast.

"Your words have merit," she finally said after several minutes. Again that predatory smile was on her lips. "However, do not make the mistake of believing all is forgiven. Until your leaders learn respect for the ways of others, you will carry my enmity. Show the others and I, that you are willing to learn the appropriate respect and we will let you go your own way." Her features began changing again, this time her head became more feline. Not the gentle appearance of today's domestic cat, but a more savage, fierce appearance. It was something that might have been the untamed ancestor of modern cats. With a polite nod, the Goddess vanished from the room, leaving behind a shimmering mist that gradually settled to the floor and became a large, dark furred cat. The feline looked up at me bright blue eyes and blinked slowly. The Goddess had left an avatar to watch us.

~ * ~

"You honestly expect me to believe this wild tale of yours."

"I know it sounds outlandish, Sir. However, it is the truth. I strongly recommend you consider your actions in this matter carefully." I glanced back at the White House.

He looked at me and shook his head slowly. "I have considered the matter carefully and my decision is made."

"Very well." I reached down and picked up the cat following behind me as the President and I walked through one of the more secluded, not that anyplace on the White House grounds was secluded, gardens.

I scratched the cat's ears gently and murmured a quiet, "I tried."

Her eyes burned darkly, and changed from their brilliant blue to black as she looked at me. *You were warned.* I heard the Goddess' voice in my mind as we walked back toward the White House.

I glanced at the President and frowned. Still scratching the cat's ears, I doubted Bast would return to her previous tactics of trying to humiliate the President. She would probably move on to something more drastic. With a silent plea to whatever deities might have been willing to listen, I asked for their blessings and protections for the world during whatever was to come.

Cave of Sorrows

The Tabeguache tell of their creation by the hand of the Creator on the slopes of the sacred mountain Tava. At the foot of this mountain was the Spirit Garden and a cave that was home to the Manitou of the Wind. All this land and the land surrounding it was home to the Tabeguache. At least it was their home until it was taken from them.

~ * ~

Soaring Eagle stood in the valley at the base of the path leading up to the cave and the home to the Manitou of the Wind. This was as far as any of the Tabeguache were allowed to approach the sacred cave—and only he, as the tribal Poowagudt was allowed into the sacred valley.

Today he was seeking counsel from the Manitou of the Wind, hoping to find a way to protect his people from the coming storm he had seen in his visions. A storm that grew as more and more of the invaders moved deeper into the Tabeguache's land. Unfortunately, there was only silence from the cave. Soaring Eagle turned to leave.

"Soaring Eagle."

The Poowagudt looked up to see a young woman standing just outside the sacred valley entrance.

"Red Feather?"

"A large band of Komatchia have been spotted. They are riding with the blue coat cavalry and are painted for war."

Soaring Eagle nodded. Now he understood why the Manitou had not spoken to him. The storm was already upon them. There was no way to stop it.

~ * ~

"So where are we?" Kelli asked.

"I'm not sure." Lucas glanced around at the trees and rock walls that surrounded the small canyon they were standing in. "We

74

were supposed to be in Colorado in what was once the United States of America on Earth."

Kelli frowned. "I know where we were supposed to be you idiot—where *are* we?"

Lucas shook his head. "I'm not sure, but I think we're in the right area." He paused, then pointed to an area to his right. "That looks like an old trail. Let's check it out."

Kelli nodded and took the lead as she picked her way through the scrub pine and underbrush.

Lucas followed his partner up the overgrown switchback trail. It led to the rim of the canyon. The area had been abandoned for several centuries. Mankind had spread out among the stars and had all but completely abandoned their home. Now, several groups had come back looking for places where they could settle. Mankind was coming home.

The climb took considerable time. The trail had washed out in places. Lucas was surprised any portion of the path remained, but realized even though they were well below the tree line, damage done to the grasses and soil, by those who once walked this path when humans were still living on Earth, could take millennia to recover. He knew there were places farther up the mountains where wagon ruts would still be part of the landscape well past the time these were finally worn away. "So where are we?" Lucas asked.

"We're supposed to be in Colorado," Kelli said, shaking her head.

Lucas smiled.

A soft breeze blew over them and Lucas froze as he let the cool air wrap itself around him. A low moan accompanied it and he laughed as Kelli spun around looking for the source of the sound.

"Looking for ghosts?" he asked.

"This is a wild place," she said as if that was the only answer that was needed.

"Wild place? Most of the Earth is now a wild place, Kelli."

"I'm not talking about those places that were the first to be abandoned. I'm talking about a truly wild place. A place where the Earth has reclaimed what once was."

Lucas shook his head. Kelli had been his partner for several years. He still didn't understand her. He had always accepted her spiritual side, yet it seemed to be taking over more and more of her thinking.

Wild places, or at least what was commonly thought of as wild places, were the places which had been abandoned first when the population had started dropping and people began leaving Earth. Most of those who had decided to not leave had moved to the larger cities.

Places once crowded became more moderately populated. Those who would have been expected to stay in places like this had been some of the first to go off planet in search of adventure and new lands.

"Probably the wind blowing across the mouth of that cave." Lucas pointed to a dark area with a stone arch outlining it. He glanced up at the darkening sky.

"Since we don't appear to be near a remaining city, perhaps we can shelter there for the night," Kelli said.

~ * ~

Soaring Eagle looked out across the valley. He could see the smoke rising. Red Feather had run back to the village while he called on the spirits to help their people. The winds had swirled, but no visions or answers had come. Now he saw Red Feather and others racing toward him, flames chasing them as they fled from the Komatchia, the blue coats and the fire.

Only a handful of women, two of the warriors and most of the older children crossed into valley. Soaring Eagle pointed to the sacred trail and followed them up the steep twisting path.

He knew there would be no forgiveness for their desecration of the sacred valley when the winds began swirling around them, driving the flames faster in pursuit of the Tabeguache. The fire blocked the trail and surrounded them in its hot embrace.

Soaring Eagle drew his knife and nodded to the two warriors and the women. They knelt down and called the children to them. They were coughing from the smoke and heat.

Soaring Eagle felt the heat intensify yet again. With prayers for their spirits, he and the other adults carefully cut the throats of the children so they would not have to endure the pain of the fire that would purify their souls for their desecration. With more prayers for forgiveness Soaring Eagle assisted the adults as well.

As the bodies of his people lay around him, Soaring Eagle knelt and raised his arms in prayer, ash falling around him as he accepted his fiery death.

~ * ~

"Do you have the porta-comp set up yet?" Kelli asked. Her voice echoed and bounced in the dark cave.

"Just got it powered up." Lucas touched several icons on the holo-screen. "Scanning for our location now."

"We're in Colorado," Kelli said. "Manitou Springs, a place called Cave of the Winds."

"How do you know that?"

She raised the flashlight she was carrying and illuminated the faded sign on the cave wall. "The low humidity and protection the cave provided preserved the sign."

"Then we're not too far from our target area." He shifted the image on the porta-comp. "We wanted a place called Colorado Springs. The map is showing Manitou Springs and Colorado Springs were next to each other. There was a major road that connected the two. We might be able to locate the road after sun up and follow it to Colorado Springs."

"Denver was the place that was supposed to be populated. Why aren't we going there?"

"We're looking for a place for our people Kelli, not a place where we have to merge into another group."

A groan came from the darkness and Kelli spun around.

"Cave of the Winds. Remember." Lucas laughed and went back to reviewing the information on the screen.

"This is a wild place. We shouldn't have stayed here."

"This cave was never a place where people lived. We'll be fine for the night. Get some sleep."

"Lucas, this is a *true* wild place. It was wild when humans still lived in this area. It has a connection to something. I just don't know what."

Lucas shivered. Kelli was scared. It worried him. "Get some sleep, Kelli. We'll be fine. I'm setting up the sensor grid." He tossed her a silver bracelet. "We'll be alerted well before anything approaches." He slipped a similar bracelet around his left wrist.

"And, we'll be leaving as soon as the sun is up."

~ * ~

Kelli woke in the pale light created by the porta-comp. The holo-screen was still active, but there was nothing displayed, just a glowing light hanging above the unit. Lucas was still asleep in his bedroll beside her.

There was another groan from deep in the cave. This time, she thought she heard a voice. *You must leave this place. It is sacred to my people.*

"Lucas!" She elbowed her partner.

Groggily he answered her. "What?"

"Listen!"

There was another groan, followed by a rushing wind and howls from the depths.

Many, many turns of the wheel ago, the white man finally left this place and it was reclaimed by those to whom it was sacred. Their spirits found a safe haven with me within my *home. Now, you have returned and again you desecrate that which is sacred, just as your people did long ago.*

"We meant no desecration, we only sought shelter from the night," Lucas said, wide awake and a bit scared.

I have heard your words and I have seen into your hearts. You seek to return to these lands which never belonged to you. When you left the Earth, the spirits were able to finally find peace and begin healing the wounds your people caused to the land. Those who belong to them will be returned when they are ready. You must leave this place.

Kelli grabbed a blanket off her bedroll and wrapped it around her shoulders as the wind began swirling around her and Lucas. More sounds came from the depths of the cave. They were becoming more and more distinct. Instead of moans and whistles, the sounds turned to screams along with numerous voices talking all together, creating a cacophony of noise that could not be understood.

"Lucas!" Kelli yelled and pointed to the cave entrance. Standing just outside the cave, moonlight shining through their bodies, were dozens of figures.

You must leave this place. The voice was now magnified as if the words had been spoken by tens of thousands.

"Lucas." Kelli pleaded. "Get us out of here. Please!"

Lucas grabbed the porta-comp and quickly typed a series of commands into the panel. Then the cave vanished and they were back on the small scout ship they had arrived in.

"You were right Kelli," Lucas said softly. "That was a wild place. One that should remain wild."

Kelli nodded and just wrapped the blanket tighter. In the last few seconds while she had stood in the swirling winds all she could hear was the sound of children crying.

~ * ~

The Tabeguache tell of their creation by the hand of the Creator on the slopes of the sacred mountain Tava. At the foot of this mountain was the Spirit Garden and a cave that was home to the Manitou of the Wind. All this land and the land surrounding it was home to the Tabeguache. At least it was until it was taken from them.

As with all things the great wheel will eventually complete its cycle and start a new one. When it does the Tabeguache will return home.

The Last Defenders

The echo of my horse's hooves on the stones of the road rings in the night. How many years have I been trapped in this half-life? How many nights have I ridden through the streets of San Antonio de Bexar? How many times have I failed to reach Travis and the others? How many times have I fallen to the rifles of Santa Anna's army unable to reach the Alamo? Unable to tell them of Fannin's treachery.

They were expecting his reinforcements and he turned back, returning to Goliad after less than a day of travel. I don't know the reason why Fannin's troops turned their backs on Travis, but Houston said holding the Alamo as long as possible was key to Texas' Independence. How much longer could they have held if Fannin's troops and artillery had reached them?

The timbre of my horse's hooves changes and I pull back on the reins—something is different. We have crossed the river and there is no sign of the Mexican Army. When I fell, all those nights ago, I was ambushed at this spot and never made it across the river. How is it that, this time, there is no ambush, no army between me and the Alamo?

I pause and stare at the field between where I sit on my horse and the front gates of the old church. Where previously the Mexican Army led by General Antonio Lopez de Santa Ana was camped, there is only grassland. But there is something else. The breeze catches the flag flying above the barracks and as it unfurls slightly, I see—not the familiar red, white and blue of the Texas flag, but the green, white and red of the Mexican flag. The battle is long over, Houston defeated Santa Anna at San Jacinto—even trapped as I am in this recurring nightmare ride, I do know what happened. How is it that a Mexican flag now flies over the Alamo?

I kick my horse lightly and he snorts, but refuses to take another step toward the Alamo. A harder kick and he neighs and rears, then takes a step back. No matter how hard I try to convince him to move, he only moves backward.

I dismount and he vanishes, but not before he taps the ground with his hoof. A sign he will be at this spot when I return. I feel myself being drawn toward the Alamo and I relax as I make my way toward the fort. I know the Mexicans who traveled with Santa Anna were superstitious and perhaps, having a ghostly presence in the Alamo will be enough to make them leave. I still remember how they tried to burn the Alamo after the battle and how several spirits appeared with flaming swords—their message was clear; they would continue to defend the Alamo. Now, that I'm a ghost, I can sense the amount of blood that has been spilled and the number of spirits laid to rest in this ground. I don't know who the spirits were who appeared, but I believe they were Travis, Bowie, Crockett and Dickenson. They were the last to defend the Alamo and would be the newest spirits in the area and the least likely to have found their rest—especially with their defeat.

A group of men have set up a small campfire near the breach where Santa Anna's men were finally able to find a way into the Alamo. I stand behind them, knowing they cannot see me. I smile as one of them glances up then quickly makes the sign of the cross over his chest. They may not be able to see me, but he at least was able to sense my presence. This was once a church and later became a fort, perhaps they understand they are desecrating hallowed ground, or perhaps they heard the stories of why Santa Anna's men refused to burn the Alamo; of the last defenders and their flaming swords.

I turn and head toward the chapel. It is the largest building on the grounds and is still relatively intact and the best place for a commander to have his headquarters. However, the best place to learn anything would be where the majority of the troops are—the barracks. I pause and turn my attention there.

~ * ~

"Madre de Dios."

"Paz?"

"Did you not sense the spirit watching us?"

The other two men laugh, a forced laugh, as they looked around at the crumbling walls. "You have been listening to Lisandro's ghost stories again. There are no spirits here—only memories."

"You are a fool." Paz pulled a silver crucifix from under his shirt and kissed it. "My cousin was one of those who was here when el Generalissimo ordered them to burn this place. He saw the diablos who stood between the army and the doors."

"And how much celebrating had he done prior to seeing these spirits?"

Paz stood and brushed the dirt from his pants. "May the angels watch over you." He paused and looked up at the stars. "Strong memories have their own power and leave a bit of themselves behind as well. Whether it was a memory or a spirit—there was a presence here. Good night."

"Good night."

~ * ~

I watch the one they called Paz head into one of the intact rooms of the barracks. He knelt before a figure of a woman holding a child—Mary. He was muttering a prayer asking her to protect him and his friends from vengeful spirits and asking her to guide those trapped here to a place where they could find their rest. He stood slowly and placed a hand on the wall to steady himself. Before he could turn away, I place a hand over his. I can feel the warmth in his flesh and the beat of his heart. It takes effort, but I am able to draw some of that warmth from him. His eyes go wide and I know he can now see me.

"Who are you?" He asks.

"One of those who are only a memory." My voice is weak and no louder than a whisper. "Why are you here?"

He shakes his head. "I do not know the General's orders. I only know we are not to leave the Alamo or be seen by those who live in the town."

I nod and pull my hand away from his and smile as he takes a deep breath and crosses himself again. He can no longer see me. I leave him there muttering another prayer for protection.

I was brought here for a reason. Perhaps it is for this reason I've been trapped as I have. Perhaps this is my chance for redemption so I can finally find rest. To find out I also need to find out why these men are here.

~ * ~

"Rider."

"Sir!" I snap to attention as I turn to face the voice behind me.

"You failed in reaching the Alamo to warn us Fannin would not be arriving as we expected and have had to relive that failure as punishment. You have been given a chance. A chance for both you and Fannin."

I stared at the ghostly figure, not sure who I am speaking to. However, I knew his words were true.

"This group is only a scout, sent by Santa Anna to test the vigilance of the Texans. No one in San Antonio has taken notice that they are here. They have recently received a dispatch from General Woll who is being sent by Santa Anna to reclaim Texas for Mexico."

"Should I alert those in the city about this?"

"No!" The figure paused, his features becoming more distinct—but still not identifiable as any particular defender. "We want them to report that Texas is open and vulnerable to attack. We want them to try to invade. We want them to learn a lesson they will never forget so they will leave Texas alone."

"What are my orders?"

"Return to Goliad and tell Fannin to bring his troops to Salado Creek. These men are leaving tomorrow and shortly after the return, another force will attempt to invade Texas. The Texas Army will be able to intercept them at Salado Creek, but they will need help. We will muster as many of those who defended the Alamo as we can who have not gone on to their rest, you will muster Fannin and others will muster those they can who fell at San Jacinto." The spirit started to fade then seemed to solidify again. "Tell Fannin we have put all blame and egos aside. We must all stand together or Texas will lose all we died for."

I salute the spirit who fades away along with the remaining walls of the Alamo. I find myself back on the bridge, my horse standing there, waiting for me, ready for the ride back to Goliad. The quarter moon is high in the night sky, though the light is muted by a thin layer of clouds. The diffuse light creates a ring around the moon and a single star shines within the ring. The Lone Star of Texas. It is a good omen.

~ * ~

I pull my horse up before the doors of Fort Defiance. The air still holds the odor of smoldering fires and burnt flesh where the Mexican army burned the bodies of Colonel Fannin and his men. When we were alive the ride between San Antonio and Goliad would have taken over a day. But now, as spirits bound to this place as well as the Alamo, it seems only seconds have passed. A quick glance at the haloed moon confirms it hasn't moved.

As I dismount, several ghostly figures form in front of the doors. Colonel Fannin steps forward from the group.

"Rider?"

"I've just returned from the Alamo and your troops are needed in San Antonio to defend Texas."

"We did our duty long ago and this was our reward." Fannin gestured to the spirits of his men and the still smoldering fires. "We were prepared to do our duty to Texas, but we received conflicting orders from those playing political games. Go to the Alamo, return to Goliad, send men to Refugio, retreat to Victoria. In the end, all we succeeded in doing was being massacred."

"I was told to tell you: We have to put all blame and egos aside. We must all stand together or Texas will lose all we died for."

I watch as Fannin stepped back and talked to his men then the group faded from site. "Damn." I turn back to my horse and start to mount, even if Fannin and his men won't come with me, I will return to San Antonio to defend Texas.

My horse neighs and bobs his head toward the doors of the Fort. There, slowly solidifying with their weapons in hand are Fannin's troops. "We will answer the call," Fannin said.

~ * ~

The sounds of battle fill the air and fog surrounds us and we find ourselves standing in a copse of trees near a creek. On one side of the creek, holding the elevated ground is a small group of Texas militia. On our side are the troops of the Mexican army; at least one thousand men plus artillery.

There are several casualties among the Mexican troops and they are realigning their remaining troops and fortifying their position. With their numbers, even with the Texas militia having the superior position, they will eventually be able to defeat the defenders. That is; unless we do something to prevent it.

There is a stirring in the air, as if lightening had struck nearby. Looking around I see more spirits appearing in the area. Men I recognize from the Alamo and others that would have been with Houston.

"Touch them," I call out. "You can draw enough strength from a person for them to see you." I touch the man I am standing next to feeling his strength flow into me. As I glance at him, I realize it is the same man I spoke to in the Alamo, Paz he was called.

His eyes go wide, but he doesn't have the same sense of fear he had before. Instead he nods his head slightly. "You and the other spirits wish us to leave Texas."

"We do." I look around; many of the soldiers are starting to back away. The acrid scent of their fear is strong. Near the back of the army and forcing his way through is a man on a horse. Another rider, next to him, carries the army's banner. This must be General Woll. He is calling orders—not yelling but speaking loudly, clearly and with authority. The soldiers are starting to regroup, their fear replaced by their discipline and respect for their general.

Another volley of shots rings out and several more of the soldiers fall. "Go," I say. "Leave this place."

Paz shakes his head and drops his gaze away from me. "I have my duty."

"And we have ours." I pull my hand away and move to where more of the spirits are gathering. There is something calling me and I feel the power growing in the area.

Six spirits appear between the soldiers and the creek, each one holding flaming swords. "Diablo's!" The name ripples through the soldiers as many of them drop to their knees and cross themselves. I look around for Paz, he is also kneeling, but it is not from fear—there is a sense of reverence and awe surrounding him. Perhaps he understands why we are here, why we are still fighting, why independence and freedom are so important.

More soldiers fall, but there were no shots fired from the Texas Militia. Behind the six spirits with the swords, another figure appears; this one larger and also holding a flaming sword. He assumes a defensive position before the members of the Texas

Militia; his meaning clear: He will defend these men from all attacks.

The general rides forward, his own sword drawn. The soldiers hesitate, but do follow him forward.

A ball of flame strikes the ground in front of the general's horse and it rears up. General Woll stays in the saddle and calms the horse enough to move forward again. Another ball of flame.

"General Woll," a voice says and echoes in the valley. "Too much blood has already been spilled and we have no desire to see more spilled. However, be warned, we will continue to defend Texas and her freedom. Leave now and you will be allowed to go in peace. Continue this invasion and you will lose. Texas no longer belongs to President Santa Anna or Mexico."

General Woll nodded then sheathed his sword. "I will concede you have the winning position here, and I do not wish to sacrifice my men in a losing battle. However, this land belongs to Mexico—you took it by force, not by right, and it will one day return to Mexico."

"Perhaps, but not as long as we remain to defend Texas and her independence."

~ * ~

General Woll ordered his troops to leave Texas and return to Mexico. Unfortunately, their return was not uneventful as a small group of cavalry attacked the Mexicans. Because we had promised General Woll he would be allowed to leave in peace, we did not stop the massacre of General Dawson and his men. And because of this our spirits have not found their final rest. We are still here, though not as trapped as we once were. All of us are here because we are defenders of Texas. We are the ones who will always be here ready to stand between Texas and those who would take freedom and independence from her or her citizens. We will not take the place of those who are alive and willing stand up, and we will always welcome new defenders into our ranks—because we are the Last Defenders.

Legends Reborn

Gwendolyn Robbins clutched the stack of papers, the wind tearing at them; trying to steal them from her grasp, as she walked through the Wildlife Foundation's maze of buildings. She paused in the relative shelter of the main administrative building and brushed her tangled black hair out of her eyes; thankful the strong winds were keeping the flying insects away for now. *Almost two hundred years and it still hasn't returned to the brilliant blue of legend,* she thought, glancing up at the brightening amethyst sky.

When she reached her office, there were at least ten notes attached to her door. *Just what I need after sitting in the analysis center all night,* she thought.

Gwendolyn shifted the stack of papers to free her right hand then began taking the yellow slips off the door. A quick glance showed several were from Tomas Whelan. She frowned slightly at his multiple invitations to dinner. She had considered going out with him a couple of times before her promotion to Director of the Genetics Department. Now, she wasn't sure she wanted to deal with the headaches that could arise from dating one of the regional coordinators. While she wasn't his supervisor, she was the one who made the decisions on which projects received priority. The risk of perceived favoritism was high. *No, it's probably not worth the headache.*

The other messages were regarding the status of various projects her department was working on. One got her attention quickly; "We Quit!" was all it said. The small bird drawn on the note showed it was from the team working on the avian project. She knew they weren't really quitting; this was just their way of making sure she read their report first thing. *As if I don't have enough to do this morning,* she thought.

"Good morning, Gwen. Did you get my note?" a voice asked behind her. Gwendolyn turned to see Tomas smiling at her.

"Good morning. I did. All six of them. The answer is still no." She shook her head and fought the smile that threatened to turn into a giggle at the crestfallen look on her friend's face.

Tomas laid a hand on his chest and took a step back. "She mocks me. I lay my heart out for her, and the lady mocks me." He dropped to one knee, clasped his hands together and held them up in a gesture of supplication. "What must I do prove myself to you, my lady?"

Gwendolyn sighed softly and decided the best way to deal with Tomas' theatrics this morning was to change the subject. "How are the wolves working out?" she asked.

"Pretty good—so far." The sandy haired coordinator stood up, dusting his dark pants off. "Looks like it may be a while before I get the proper balance of predator to prey, but I think it's a good start."

"Glad to hear it. It's nice to know something may be working right for a change." Gwendolyn shifted the stack of papers again as she reached for her door.

"Allow me." Tomas said, opening the door and giving her a bow.

"Thanks," Gwendolyn said, walking into the office and dropping the papers on the desk.

"What's all that?" Tomas asked, gesturing at the papers.

"The animal census reports. I only have a few days before my presentation to the Council. They're trying to shut the Foundation down. They claim we're interfering and upsetting the Balance! Like there was a Balance for us to upset!" Gwendolyn clenched her fists for a moment then relaxed.

"So the rumors are true," Tomas said.

"I'm afraid so," she whispered.

Tomas reached up and gently squeezed her shoulder. "Have you considered that they may be right? We do interfere with the Balance and the natural recovery," he said.

"The natural recovery?" Gwendolyn pulled away from the coordinator. "We've tried that. It's really working isn't it?" She jerked the curtains in her office open to reveal the pale purple of the morning sky. "The damage done to the ecology of this planet in the last war is too severe for us to just sit here and do nothing!"

"By the Balance! Do you realize what you're saying?"

"Yes, I do. Do you really know what *The Balance* is? True Balance can only come when everything becomes a part of the ecology of this planet." She crossed her arms across her chest and stared at her friend. "The Council still clings to those draconian capital punishment laws for interference in the Balance, but man is a part of nature and a part of the ecology. We should never presume to dominate this planet and its resources the way the Ancestors did, but neither should we completely withdraw either." She turned and walked over to the window. "That's what we're doing, and it's destroying us. Mankind is disappearing from this planet," she whispered.

"If that's what the Balance decrees, do we have a right to say otherwise?" Tomas asked.

"We may not be able to say otherwise, but are you willing to just give up without at least trying?" she asked turning back to face him.

Tomas glanced up at her, and Gwendolyn was pleased to see a look of determination in his gray-blue eyes. "No, I suppose I'm not," he said. "If you need any help getting your presentation ready, let me know."

"I appreciate that." She smiled softly.

"Do yourself a favor, Gwen. Stop pushing so hard. Take some time for yourself." He reached up and caressed her cheek, then turned to leave.

Tomas stopped at the door and turned to face her, a crooked grin on his face. "By the way, don't think I'm going to stop trying to get you to go out with me."

"You keep trying. Maybe I'll give in out of pity one of these days," she said, smiling.

"Pity? Okay, I'll take pity. At least it's a place to start. How about tonight? I know this great cook, and his place has wonderful atmosphere," he said.

"Nice try, but I'm not quite to the pity stage yet." She gestured to the papers scattered across her desk.

"Maybe next time. Oh, before I forget, how's your pegasus project going?"

"I'll be releasing my first pair into the Foundation's habitat tonight," she said. Something that constantly surprised her about Tomas was his ability to change the subject of a conversation and his mood quickly. In many ways, he reminded her of the wolves they had recently reintroduced into his region. He had a very playful but mercurial nature and could be deadly serious when he chose.

"But, how? You just got initial approval. How can you have a pair ready for release that quickly?"

Gwendolyn looked at the door, still standing partially open, and Tomas reached back and shut it completely.

Gwendolyn grinned. "After I prepared the proposal, I went ahead and tested the material and data by developing the first pair. Meet me after work and I'll show you the pegasi."

"See you then," he said, turning and leaving the room.

Gwendolyn stared at the closed door for a few minutes surprised and a little disappointed he hadn't seized the opportunity to ask her out to dinner again. After all, she had given him a perfect opening by asking him to meet her after work. While she knew all the logical reasons to not get involved in a relationship with Tomas, she still enjoyed the attention.

She glanced down at the papers now scattered across her desk then out the window at the lavender sky. *What's the point of being involved in a relationship anyway?* She grabbed the curtains and yanked them shut. *Fewer couples are succeeding in childbearing, and only a few of those actually born survive infancy.* Gwendolyn picked up Tomas' notes. "Besides, a lover is just one more person to lose in the next famine or plague." She placed the notes in a wooden box on her windowsill. As she closed the lid, her fingers carefully traced the rearing unicorn inlayed on it in silver. *A hope chest,* she thought, *that's what Tomas called this once. Pandora's box is more like it.*

Gwendolyn sat at her desk and read the remaining notes. There was nothing that required her immediate attention, so she set them aside and picked up the report folder. As she had expected, the news was bad. For the past five years, the Foundation had been working to reintroduce various bird species. Despite the availability of genetic material in facilities like this one, all of their cloning efforts had failed.

The continuing damage to vital food crops from insects, coupled with the ban on the use of pesticides made this project a priority. At least in her opinion, it was a priority. The rising mortality rates across the planet should have made it one for the Council as well, but they seemed to be taking a wait and see attitude with the situation. Then again, they had given initial approval to her pegasus project, which was a little more proactive than she would have expected. True, the Council had withheld final approval pending the reports from the test stage, but this was more than she had actually hoped for considering the Council's decisions in the past.

The report contained no significant information from the group's recent search of the archives, except for a brief note from one of the junior members.

"Director Robbins, I believe the problem may be with the atmosphere. The birds we are able to clone all appear to be demonstrating respiratory problems. I found a reference in one of the records, which indicated birds were once used to detect the presence of dangerous gasses. Based on this, and I realize it isn't much, I would surmise birds have very sensitive respiratory systems.

"With the changes in the atmosphere after the war, it's possible all the birds died before they could adapt, as other species have. Just a thought—Jayson."

Gwendolyn pulled the curtains open and looked out the window again, shook her head and silently cursed the Ancestors and this mix and match world they had created with their last war. All over the planet, equipment sat in lifeless testament to knowledge lost or incomplete.

During the past century, mankind had begun trying to claim a small niche on the planet. Technology was being salvaged and brought together in various locations. One of these was the Wildlife Foundation. This had been some kind of genetic facility prior to the war and there were samples of genetic material from thousands of creatures stored here. Unfortunately, all they were able to use properly was the cloning equipment. Perhaps, if the knowledge hadn't been lost they might have found a way to adapt birds to the current atmosphere. However, even if they could, that would only help with one symptom of a larger problem. She picked up her papers and moved to the adjoining conference room.

A large map covered one wall of the room, and papers were scattered across the floor and table. She glanced up from the papers she was carrying and scanned the map with its multicolored pins and ribbons. The different colors of the pins indicated different species groups, while the ribbons showed their growth patterns. Black ribbons attached to the blue pins showed clearly the status of the avian species. There were no recorded populations anywhere in the world. Green ribbons attached to green pins showed the population increases for insects. Most of the remaining pins held red ribbons, showing population decreases. Here and there were pins with no ribbons; an indication there had been no significant changes in that species' numbers.

She shifted through the papers, found the reports for each of the various regions, and began comparing the numbers from the previous and the current census. Every few seconds she found herself adding another red ribbon to a pin, which previously had held no ribbon. Only occasionally did she find herself reaching for a green ribbon or removing a red ribbon.

She finally stepped back and surveyed the map, shaking her head at the amount of red. Her eyes searched out the gold pins she used to designate humans then closed them against the tears she felt coming. Her map confirmed what she had told Tomas - humanity was dying. Based on her projections, Gwendolyn doubted mankind had many more years left to it.

Her thoughts were interrupted as Tomas burst into the office. "Gwen!"

"Calm down. What's wrong?" she asked, reaching for the papers she had dropped.

"Director Banks is on his way here with members of the Council." He started gathering up the papers scattered on the floor and table.

Gwendolyn stood frozen, staring at her friend. "What? Why?"

"Don't know. But they didn't look happy." He finished picking up the last of the papers and looked up. "Where do you want these?"

"Huh?" She shook her head slightly. "Thanks. Just put them on my desk." She nodded toward the door to her office.

"Ms. Robbins," a voice said from the doorway.

Gwendolyn looked up to see Brian Banks, the Director for the Wildlife Foundation standing in the room next to a petite woman with dark red hair and brilliant blue eyes. "Director Banks, President Kerchner. What can I do for you?"

Helen Kerchner, the President of the World Council, stepped

forward and smiled softly. "Ms. Robbins, we need to talk. The Council and I have some concerns.

"Of course." Gwendolyn gestured to the chairs around the table.

"Ms. Robbins, I have reviewed your proposal regarding your pegasus projects as well as the other *interesting* projects you have suggested. I must admit that while your ideas are intriguing, I have some reservations."

"Madam President, over the past two years, teams from the Foundation have managed to catalog every species known to still exist on Earth. My proposal deals with those ecological niches that are severely under populated or not populated at all. I believe it's possible, through cloning of unique species to fill those niches and thereby restore Balance."

"So we were correct," President Kerchner said leaning back in her chair and crossing her arms over her chest. "You are talking about creating new species. Ms. Robbins, I am sure you know the policy of the World Council is to allow for natural recovery, with minimal interference from man."

"Your proposals are a serious violation of that policy, as I have already told you," Director Banks said.

Gwendolyn met the intense gaze of his dark eyes and wasn't surprised to see nothing reflected in them. No light, no emotion—just two deep pools of black space. "I understand that," she said. "However, you need to understand it has been two centuries since the war that nearly destroyed this planet?" She turned her attention back to the Council President. "Every day we are still reminded of that event. Records say the sky was once as blue as your eyes. In the time since the war, it still has not returned to that color. The Balance has not been restored. Moreover, it will never be restored if man is not considered as part of the equation. Two hundred years and mankind is afraid to do anything that might risk the ecological balance of the Earth. We live in constant fear of making a mistake and destroying what life is left."

"With good reason, I'd say. Look around you at what is left." President Kerchner leaned forward, her blue eyes piercing in their intensity.

"You look around!" Gwendolyn slapped her hands against the table. "Man has hung on by the skin of his teeth since the war.

We are afraid to live. We are unwilling to be a part of the Balance anymore, and it's killing us." She gestured to the map covering the walls. For the next several minutes, she carefully explained about the colored pins and ribbons.

"While, I have not completed all the comparisons yet, you can still see from the amount of red on the map, populations have declined since last year. The Council has got to realize what's happening. This planet is dying! New methods must be explored."

"Perhaps, but that is not your decision to make." The President's eyes narrowed slightly and she stood slowly. "I must warn you Ms. Robbins to tread carefully, the Council will be watching you closely." With a final glance at the map, she turned and left the room, Director Banks following her.

~ * ~

Gwendolyn sat on the floor of the conference room, staring at the map and occasionally glancing down at the papers in her hand. *There has to be a way to get through to them,* she thought.

Her eyes kept darting across the maps, the various colored pins with the attached red, green and black ribbons. The pin groupings within each of the regions showed the various population centers. Something didn't look right as she continued to study the map. The ratio of green and red pins in the western region of the North American continent was different from the rest of the map. She set the charts for the western region aside so she could reconstruct that area of the map later.

Let's start with these, she thought, removing the blue pins with the black ribbons. *We're all aware of the status of the avian population.* She stepped back and studied the groupings. *Okay, now for the insects.*

All of the appropriate pins and ribbons removed, Gwendolyn stepped back and looked at the map again. There were still a few green pins left in the scattered clusters. She reached for one to remove it then stopped; her hand frozen as she stared at the green dot surrounded by a rainbow of colors. There was no ribbon attached to it. Could she have forgotten? It didn't seem likely. Gwendolyn picked up her charts and flipped through them looking for the census numbers for this particular area. There it was— No significant increase or decrease in insect population.

"No significant increase or decrease in insect population," she said. "No significant increase or decrease in insect population!" She repeated the phrase like a mantra.

Gwendolyn returned her attention to the section of the map with the green pin. All of the remaining pins in that grouping were either empty or had a green ribbon attached to them. She circled the area with a green marker.

For several hours, Gwendolyn carefully checked every cluster of pins, circling those that showed characteristics similar to the first group. "Is there a pattern?" she asked herself, when she was finally done.

Gwendolyn removed every pin cluster that wasn't circled, then stepped back and smiled. All of the remaining clusters were grouped together around a central area. *It's almost like a mushroom ring surrounding an oak tree*, she thought.

Gwendolyn's thoughts were interrupted as the door to her office opened. She turned to see Tomas entering the room.

"Gwen," Tomas said. He paused as he looked around the room, his eyes wide at the papers scattered across the floor. "Work was over hours ago. And, you promised to let me meet the pegasi tonight."

"Give me a minute, then we'll go." Gwendolyn jotted down some notes on her charts then motioned to the door.

~ * ~

Gwendolyn led the way through the bare corridors to a large room set up as a habitat, similar to the woods surrounding the center. As they entered the area, two large gray wolves bounded out of the trees. "Hello, you two," Gwendolyn said as the two creatures sniffed at her and Tomas.

The two wolves followed closely as she led Tomas over to large enclosure.

"Back off you two. Sit and stay," Gwendolyn told the two wolves.

The two large canines cocked their heads at her, but both backed up several steps and sat watching her closely as she opened the enclosure. Gwendolyn smiled at the gasp she heard from Tomas when the two small black horses pranced out into the habitat. The pegasi were about three quarters the size of the wolves.

Gwendolyn brought one of them over for Tomas to see. "This is Artemis. The male is Apollo," she said. "As you can see, they look like horses in every detail; other than the obvious difference in size, that is. Other differences: They have hollow bones like a bird. And, most importantly, they like insects in addition to grass."

The two wolves looked at the pegasus still standing by the cage. One of them glanced up at Gwendolyn, and then pounced at the winged horsed in front of it. Gwendolyn laughed as Apollo jumped into the air and whinnied at the wolf. "And, they can fly. I'm sorry Remus, but it won't be easy to catch one of these guys." She reached down and scratched the wolf's ears.

"An interesting idea, Gwen. You may have come up with a solution to the avian problem. Do you think it'll work?" Tomas gave Artemis a pat.

"I hope so. The data from the Ancestors says it will." Gwendolyn let her voice trail off.

"But?" Tomas asked.

"But, it doesn't make sense. The digestive systems between a bird and a horse are so different and technically these guys shouldn't even be able to fly."

"Guess nobody ever told them they couldn't," Tomas said.

"Perhaps." Gwendolyn gently tossed Artemis up and watched as she spread her wings catching the air and gracefully glided away from them.

Gwendolyn and Tomas stood and watched the pegasi dart around the habitat, playing with each other and the two wolves.

"Gwen, what do you know about unicorns?" Tomas asked after several minutes.

She hesitated for several moments before answering. "I've studied a few of the legends. Other than that, not much."

"Did you find any evidence here the Ancestors may have developed or tried to develop unicorns?"

There was a note of suspicion in Tomas' voice. "Why do you ask?"

"Director Banks asked me to research several unicorn sightings and I discovered that they center around a central location. The area of the Foundation." Tomas reached out and took her hands in his. "Gwen, I need to know. Are you the one responsible for the unicorns?"

Gwendolyn stared at her friend for a few minutes, searching his face for an indication of his true motives in asking that question. Tomas had staunchly supported the Council decisions regarding non-interference in the natural recovery processes in the past. Would he be open minded enough to understand something she wasn't sure she understood herself?

Gwendolyn turned back to watch the pegasi as they glided to the ground. The two wolves trotted over and the four animals touched noses. "No," she whispered. "However, I do have a theory as to where they might have come from. Follow me." She led the way out of the habitat building to the genetics labs.

"The Ancestors experimented with the idea of creating animals from mythology. They left behind research and genetic material from numerous species, including the pegasi and unicorns. The Council has tightly controlled most of this information. Only Brian and I have had access."

"I guess that's why no one could figure out where you got the materials for the pegasi."

Gwendolyn only smiled as she looked at Tomas, then turned toward the computer. "It took a while, but I was finally able to get into the system and begin cataloguing the work the Ancestors were doing." She pushed several buttons and the image of a rearing unicorn appeared on the screen. "These are the files and records I was able to recover. Unfortunately, they are not complete. From what I have been able to find, the Ancestors created test subjects for all of the creatures listed in this database."

"Any indications they took their experiments further than the test phase?" Tomas stood behind her and placed a strong hand on her shoulder.

"Not that I could find. However, these may only be the preliminary records. Although, it seems the primary focus here was on unicorns. I personally believe the Ancestors did create and release unicorns."

Tomas sighed deeply then stepped back. Gwendolyn turned to face him. He stood with his arms crossed across his chest and a faraway look in his eyes. "Just what information do you have on the unicorns?"

"They were solitary creatures, very elusive, almost impossible to find. The pool a unicorn drank from would be pure and clean. The areas where they lived were green and fertile with abundant plant and animal life. And lastly, they were the guardians and bringers of hope." She paused and glanced from the unicorn on the screen to Tomas and back.

"Guardians and bringers of hope," Gwendolyn said suddenly. "Come on! I want to check something." She jumped up and hurried back to main building.

~ * ~

"Gwen, what's going on?" Tomas demanded when they got back inside, out of the howling wind.

Gwendolyn brushed her hair back from her face and took several deep breaths before answering. "I can't really explain it. I'll have to show you. Do me a favor. Get your notes on the unicorn sightings and meet me in my office."

Tomas raised his eyebrows and frowned slightly, then nodded. "Sure."

After entering her office, Gwendolyn got a box of silver pins from her desk then went into the conference room.

"Here's the unicorn information. Now, will you please tell me what's going on?" Tomas said, handing her a folder.

"In a few minutes. Let me check something first." Gwendolyn handed the folder back to Tomas. "Read me the locations on each of those sightings."

Tomas sighed, shook his head slightly, and then opened the folder.

As he read off each location, Gwendolyn marked each one on the map with a silver pin. When they were done with all of the reports, there was at least one silver pin in all of the circled clusters.

"I knew it!" Gwendolyn said.

"Knew what?" Tomas asked, staring at her.

"All of these areas are showing stabilization or growth. I first noticed they had no significant increase or decrease in their insect populations. Further checking showed the other groups demonstrated either the same or population increases. There was no significant decrease in any species group—including man. Now, we find *all* of the reported unicorn sightings are in these areas. There has to be a connection!"

Tomas studied the map for a moment. "I agree it appears that way. But, what exactly is the connection?" he asked.

"Legends call unicorns the guardians and bringers of hope. Could it be that simple? Is what's needed be something as simple as hope?" Gwendolyn asked, staring at the silver pins. "Or were the Ancestors able to actually breed for magic?"

"There are a lot of the old technologies, we don't understand. Perhaps they weren't breeding for magic, precisely. However, they could have given the unicorns some sort of ability that allows them to influence the plants and animals in an area to promote healing and balance. To us it might look like magic." He reached forward and placed his hand next to one of the silver pins. "Besides, does it really matter? What matters is something is happening and the unicorns may be the catalyst."

"So, what should we do about it? Do we report this to the Council or ignore it for now?"

"We definitely don't ignore it, but we don't report it; at least not yet. Once we have enough information on the changes that are occurring, combined with the current and previous census reports, we will be able to show the Council what's going on. And, they *will* have to listen to you. But, before we do that there must be no doubt regarding the unicorns and their influence."

"Tomas, you've have always supported the Council, why would you suggest this?" She backed away a few steps.

"Because, I believe you're right. The unicorns could be just a coincidence, but I doubt it. I've seen the previous census reports. I know what's been happening to the various species groups on this planet. Something has to be done. The fact the Council gave you preliminary approval for your pegasi, shows they are more aware of what's happening than we give them credit for."

Tomas placed his hands on Gwendolyn's shoulders and squeezed gently. "Come on," he said. "It's getting late and we both need to get some rest. I'll walk you home."

"Thank you," she said softly as they left the room.

~ * ~

Outside the administrative building a flash of silver and gold caught Gwendolyn's eye. "Did you see that?" she whispered.

"I did. Do you think…?" Tomas let his voice trail off.

"I want to. We could use some hope around here."

There was another flash of silver and a soft whinny echoed in the trees, followed by a rhythmic drumming.

Gwendolyn smiled at Tomas as the sounds faded into the night. "Perhaps magic is nothing more than hope and a belief in things hoped for," she said.

"If that's true, there may already be magic in the world," Tomas said.

Gwendolyn only nodded as they walked down the path.

Time of the Month

All those men running around with swords, I knew someone was going to get hurt. What I didn't know was that it was going to be me.

Krystall paused as she approached the doors to Duke Jucaysa's hall. All she had done was ask what was causing the near panic when she entered the town gates and the next thing she knew a group of guardsmen were telling her the Duke wanted to see her. Apparently someone had pointed her out as being the warrior who had slain the dragon Gramudyus; and since everyone was concerned about the appearance of another dragon, the Duke believed she was the one to handle it.

As far as Krystall was concerned, they needed to find someone else. It had been fifteen years since she fought Gramudyus. She was feeling her age as well as all the leagues she had traveled. What she wanted right now was a hot bath, a hot meal and a relaxing drink. Then to hole up for about a week.

"Ah, Krystall, Sword Maiden of Malytta. I welcome you to my hall." The Duke stood and extended his arms.

Krystall frowned. She hated that title. Some other Duke had given it to her. Then, he'd promptly commissioned a bard to write the tale his daughter's rescue from a dark mage. Still the tale usually earned her a free meal and several drinks in taverns when someone realized she was the one being sung about. Having a reputation did have a few perks. Of course, the downside was everyone wanted you to solve their problems for them, regardless of whether you wanted to or not.

Besides, she definitely wasn't a maiden.

She smiled and bowed her head slightly as she studied the Duke. He was an older man, maybe a year or two younger than she was. However, while her hair was still full and black, his was thin and gray. His brown eyes were dull and his face was weathered and lined. Based on the threadbare cloak he was wearing, and the lack of adornments on him or in the hall, this was one of the poorer areas of the realm.

"My Lord." She paused, choosing her next words with care. "May I know the reason I was brought here?"

"My apologies for the abruptness in summoning you here." He gestured to a nearby bench. "As you saw when you arrived, things are a bit confused. The dragon Freynia has been holding our town hostage for many years and has demanded we pay her a steep tribute each year. Recently, a traveling seer told us Freynia would be vulnerable during the two days before the moon is at its fullest." He paused and took a breath. "Many of the men in this town think to be the ones to dispatch the dragon. However, none of them have the training or skills to do so."

"And…," She waited.

"And, with your reputation…." He swallowed hard then looked down at the floor. "I was hoping to hire you to slay Freynia for us."

"Sorry, but this is not a good time." Was it ever not a good time, but men never understood these things. "I doubt I'm up to handling dragons anymore. I would be willing to give some training and advice to the person who goes after her. She turned toward the door. "It won't be me."

"Please."

Krystall hesitated. She heard the Duke's desperation. *Why do I always have to be a sucker for hopeless causes.* She turned back to face the Duke.

"I know it doesn't look like we can offer much, but I will grant you half of the dragon's hoard, which should be considerable, considering the number of years she has been blackmailing us," he said. "As well as anything else you want that is within my power to give you." His right hand was wrapped around in his left.

Krystall looked at the Duke. She almost expected him to drop to his knees and beg the way his hands were now rubbing each other.

"If the hoard is as big as you say it is, I only lay claim to one quarter of it. From the looks of this place, your people need it more than I do."

"Thank…"

She held up her hand. "I'm not finished."

"If it is within my power."

"I want a place to retire. Where I can be left *alone*."

"I will grant you a landholding within my domain. And, a title befit...,"

"No!" Her hand went to her sword. "No more titles. Just a small place—not too far from here, but as isolated as possible."

"I will review the maps and will find you several locations to choose from."

She let a heartbeat pass before she spoke. "Where do I find this Freynia?"

"She makes her lair to the east, near one of the older emerald mines. It is about two days ride."

"Two days." Might be enough time. "And this traveling seer told you Freynia would be most vulnerable during the two days before the moon is full."

"He did."

"That gives me a day to get ready before leaving," she said. "Do you have an herb-witch in this town?"

"Herb-witch? I am not familiar with the term."

"I will introduce you to the one I consult with," a soft voice said from behind the Duke.

"My Lady." Krystall inclined her head slightly as an older woman stepped from the shadows and stood next to the Duke. Like her husband, the Lady wore a threadbare cloak and her face, though it still reflected the beauty of her youth, was lined. Her green eyes sparkled as she smiled.

The Duchess stepped forward and held out her hand. "Come with me. I will show you your chamber so you can rest."

Krystall nodded and followed her hostess out of the room.

~ * ~

Krystall grimaced. The morning sun cut through the clouds, creating shimmering mirages in the distance. Her abdomen was in knots from the stronger than normal mixture the herb-witch had given her. The witch had explained the timing was too close. The normal mixture wouldn't work properly.

However, she hadn't been sure this would work either. Now after two days of travel, her insides were protesting and she *still* had a dragon to deal with.

"Why did I agree to this?" she growled.

She patted her horse's neck and surveyed the area. Even though everyone only talked about her defeat of Gramudyus, she had fought an even dozen dragons in her life, and probably understood them better than anyone else.

This Freynia made her lair in the remains of an emerald mine. Krystall had no doubt the dragon would have made use of the tunnels to create numerous exits. The question was, which one did she favor as her main route into and out of the lair, and which ones might she have forgotten about?

As her gaze moved over the area, she spotted a large open tunnel entrance and nodded. That was the one the dragon wanted others to think was the main one.

She continued to scan the area. There behind a group of boulders was another entrance. The edges of the boulders were worn and there was a sheen to them that showed where the dragon had rubbed against them as she came and went.

She continued to study the area, but found no other signs of possible other tunnels. Now that was very odd. The last dragon she had fought, Leystav, had been young, but he still had over twenty maze like tunnels into his lair. Gramudyus had almost a hundred. It had taken her three months to find all the entrances and study them before she had been willing to tackle the ancient dragon.

Kyrstall guided her horse to a sheltered area behind some weathered boulders and tethered the mare there.

Perhaps she wouldn't need to worry about the other entrances if the dragon was supposed to be vulnerable, like the seer had told Duke Jucaysa.

A wolf howled in the distance. She felt a chill wrap itself around her heart at the painful sound.

Making sure her horse could free herself if necessary, Kyrstall headed for the dragon's lair.

~ * ~

Part of her secret in fighting dragons was a charm. It helped her eyes adjust to the tunnel darkness. She didn't need to announce her presence by carrying a torch or lantern.

Another howl stopped her. The sound echoed in the tunnel. Similar to the wolf she had heard outside, but with a deepness reminding her of a dragon's roar. She frowned. There was something else in the sound. She listened. It choked off into a painful whimper.

What, by all the Lords of Chaos, is going on here?

She drew her sword, cringing at the soft scraping as it came out of the scabbard. There were no other sounds from the tunnel and she continued on her way.

The tunnel widened and she stopped. Her breath caught as she stared at the creature. Lying in the large black walled chamber was the dragon. Only it wasn't a dragon-not any more.

Her stomach twisted.

The dragon was caught in the midst of a wolf shape change.

Freynia had curled up as tightly as her dragon body would allow. Her scales had patchy fur and her legs looked like a dog's but shiny. She looked up at Krystall, then dropped her head back on the stone floor. A barking hiss escaped her fanged mouth.

Krystall shook her head. She lifted her sword and cautiously approached the dragon. This was *not* the way one of these great reptiles should be killed.

She raised her sword and glanced down at Freynia's golden eyes. The dragon blinked once, then nodded her head. Not taking her luck for granted, she drove the sword hard into the dragon's chest, then twisted the blade as she pulled it out.

The dragon's lips curled as her eyes closed. The transformation stopped. The dragon returned to her own form.

"May the great mother of dragons spread her wings over you," Krystall whispered.

"Nicely done."

Krystall spun around, her sword held ready. An older man with long gray hair and matching beard, dressed in silver robes stood there. His blue eyes twinkled as his gaze moved past her to where the dragon's hoard was piled against a far rock wall.

"Peace," he said. "I am here to recover something that belonged to me. Nothing more." He stepped past her, not looking down as his robes rustled against the dragon's scales.

Krystall waited as the man reached into the pile of coins, gems and other trinkets and removed a staff. Topping the carved wood was the figure of a wolf's head; the nose raised and mouth opened to howl.

"Taken from me a few weeks ago, shortly after the last full moon. A very foolish bit of thievery on her part." He glanced at the dragon's body and shook his head.

Now she knew who the seer was. "You're the one who told Duke Jucaysa she would be vulnerable at this time?"

"I am." He bowed his head slightly. "I am known as the Wolf Seer and this creature came to me with a question. She didn't like my answer and stole my staff because of it."

"If I may ask, what was the question?"

The old man smiled. "She wanted to know how to gain true immortality. It is the one thing dragons seek." His fingers tightened on the staff. "They know they can never have it."

She glanced back at the still body and nodded. Despite their long lives, dragons were not truly immortal. Some had been known, or so she had heard, to offer their entire hoard to any mage who could grant them true immortality. None had ever achieved it.

"Why did she seek you out?"

"I am the Wolf Seer. I asked the pack and the other creatures of this area to spread the story I had learned the secret to dragon immortality."

"Why?"

"Because I had an answer for her." He straightened his back and raised his chin, as if daring her to challenge what he said.

"What did you tell her?"

"That to gain the only form of true immortality, she would have to die in battle, at the hand of a true warrior."

"What nonsense is that?" Krystall stared at the seer and shook her head. "To gain immortality she had to die? Where is the immortality in that?"

"It is the same immortality you share with Leystav and Gramudyus. The only true immortality there is, he paused, "to live forever in story and song." His staff glowed.

Krystall raised her head. A low howl echoed into the room.

"Even though I can call the wolves, there is no danger to you," he reassured her. "I am the Wolf Seer and I run with the pack."

The glow faded and the old man vanished. Standing in front of her was a large dark gray wolf. The staff shimmered then flowed around the wolf creating a twig collar around his neck.

She held out the back of her hand and the wolf touched his wet nose lightly to it before he trotted out of the chamber.

Krystall sheathed her sword and looked at the dragon's treasure. She only had one horse and it was a two-day ride back to Duke Jucaysa, then another two days back here, if she wanted more. She filled a sack with various gems and headed out of the cave.

Her stomach twisted into a knot and she almost doubled over from the pain. *I hate this time of the month,* she thought as she mounted her horse and headed back.

A Story of Inyodo

or

How the Kappa Stole the Tidal Jewels from the Dragon King

Late one night one of the troublesome kappa looked down on the island of Japan and smiled in that mischievous and somewhat scary manner only those who are up to no good can smile in.

"It has been many turnings of the seasons since these people have seen a change in their fortunes. For too long has Fuku Riu favored them and now they no longer understand the blessing they are receiving."

The kappa spoke to his kindred and together they developed a plan to change the fortunes of the people of Japan. The kappa would steal the Tidal Jewels belonging to Ryujin, the Dragon King, and use them to cause a tidal wave to strike the island of Japan. It would not be enough to completely destroy the island, but would remind the people to give thanks for the blessings the gods had bestowed on them.

Being only a minor demon, the kappa only saw things in absolute terms. The gods blessed the people of Japan after the devastation they had suffered during their last war. They had rebuilt and were now a wealthy and powerful people. Wealth and power many of them seemed to take for granted—forgetting Fuku Riu, the luck dragon, blessed them and luck could change on a whim.

The kappa and four of his kin descended to the Evergreen Land beneath the sea and came to Ryugu—the palace of the Dragon King Ryujin. The crystal and coral palace was immense, but they were determined to find the Tidal Jewels. Of the five kappa, one went directly to the throne room of the Dragon King while each of the others went to the cardinal wings of the palace: North, South, East and West as none of them knew where the Tidal Jewels were kept.

The first kappa came to the Winter Hall and paused at the beauty of the falling snow. Forgetting why he was there, he began playing and cavorting in the winter playground—throwing snowballs at imaginary enemies.

The second kappa came to the Hall of Spring and wandered among the cherry trees with their pink blossoms, entranced by the music of the nightingale that filled the hall.

The third kappa came to the Hall of Summer. There the warm night breeze and the songs of the crickets lulled him into slumber.

The fourth kappa came to the Autumn Hall and was soon dancing among the beautiful multi-colored leaves of the towering maple trees.

The fifth kappa came to the great hall of the Dragon King and stopped at the entrance. Ryujin was sitting on his crystal throne and there on the arms of the chairs were the Tidal Jewels. He watched as the Dragon King glanced up at the image of the moon that was on the ceiling of the palace and carefully stroked one of the jewels. The kappa closed his eyes for a moment and let his senses feel the magic. It had been the high tide jewel Ryujin used. This was the one the kappa wanted, but how to get it away from the Dragon King.

The kappa glanced around the room, which, as expected for a dragon, was cluttered with treasures and trinkets collected for millennia. He had heard a rumor Huchi had given Ryujin her ring made of fire to guard his palace. With that ring, the kappa knew he could distract Ryujin and then steal the Tidal Jewels.

Ryujin looked toward the entrance to his hall and the kappa darted into the stacks of treasures. Where to find the ring made of fire he wondered. The dragon King had been collecting treasure for millennia—most of it from ships lost beneath the waters of his ocean. However, some of it had been offered as tribute or gifts by fishermen and sailors and others had been given as gifts of friendship or alliance as with Huchi's ring.

The kappa knew the ring gave protections to the palace so he doubted it was thrown haphazardly in with the rest of the items. It was fire contained by powerful magic; he should be able to sense it. There, no wait, there. The kappa found himself spinning around as the magic seemed to surround him. A ring made of fire. The Ring of Fire—now the kappa understood.

He wished his kin were with him as the five of them would be able to more easily accomplish what he was about to do. He concentrated, focusing his magic on the Ring of Fire. Just a nudge should be enough to cause a minor quake. Just enough to distract the Dragon King and draw him away from the Tidal Jewels.

The palace shook and the kappa heard Ryujin roar. He ran as objects began falling around him, the shaking growing in power. He ducked behind a large chest as the dragon king flew past him and out of the palace.

The jewels were unguarded and the kappa knew this was his chance. He paused in front of the throne as the shaking continued to grow in strength. Perhaps the quake would be enough to accomplish his goal. There came another rumbling of power, unbalancing the kappa who grabbed for the arm of the throne to steady himself. His hand dropped on top of the high tide jewel and it glowed brightly.

"What have you done?"

The kappa spun around to see Ryujin standing in the doorway. The dragon had adopted his guise as an elderly human male; a disapproving look on his face.

"I am reminding these humans to be thankful for the blessings they were given."

Ryujin shifted back into his dragon form, steam seeping from his lips. "You thought you would take it upon yourself to interfere in the lives of the mortals we are supposed to protect?" The dragon lowered his head until his gaze was level with the kappa's. "You would tell Fuku Riu he should withdraw his blessing? Only he can decide when it is time for their luck to change—not you!"

The kappa cringed as he was surrounded by steam and fire.

"Go—see what you have done." Ryujin's voice echoed throughout the palace.

~ * ~

The kappa looked down on the island of Japan and for the first time in his long life he cried. The force of the tsunami he created devastated the area it had hit. Instead of reminding the people of Japan to give thanks for the blessings their gods had given them, he had given them reason to curse their gods.

He saw Fuko Riu also crying. The grief and despair of the mortals was taking a heavy toll on the luck dragon as he circled the island trying to restore the balance destroyed by the kappa's actions.

The kappa flew to Hachiman's palace; he was the protector of the Japanese people. Surely he would be able to do something about this disaster the kappa had created. Many of the other gods were there, also demanding Hachiman do something to stop the disaster that had befallen their people.

The kappa was disappointed as Hachiman turned him and the others away, saying because the kappa was a deity, however minor he might be, the other gods could not reverse what he had done. They could assist the Japanese people as their powers allowed, but they could not change what the kappa had done.

The kappa looked down at the island. His simple idea of sending a tsunami to remind the Japanese people to give thanks to the gods for the blessings they had been given had brought extreme disaster. Now the full consequences of his impetuous actions were becoming clear as another, even greater disaster loomed. The mortals were fighting valiantly to prevent that disaster, but he could see their strength and faith were failing. What could he do to help them? The other gods were blessing the island as their powers allowed, but would it be enough? He was a minor deity with no strong powers, except to cause mischief—what could he bless them with that would help?

The kappa smiled again, not the devious smile of one who wishes to cause mischief, but a sincere smile. He remembered the stories the gods told of an ancient power that was reborn several years ago, during another disaster—perhaps he could persuade that power to visit Japan and bless these people as he had blessed others throughout the millennia.

The kappa concentrated on calling that power, a gift to all mortals from another group of gods. The kirin that appeared before the kappa shimmered with a silver light. "We are the bringers of justice and luck to those who are just," the kirin said lowering his horn. "Now you have given us a new purpose in times like this. We will bring hope."

The kappa found himself staring into the sun-flecked eyes of the kirin just as the horn found his heart.

"You have been judged guilty of your crime against the mortals," the kirin said. "Justice has been dealt, now hope can prevail."

Mr. Zombie Goes to Washington

It's not that hard being a zombie. Rumors of the zombie apocalypse as well as numerous books and movies made people more and more aware of the dangers zombies posed. If they actually cared to believe we existed at all. Most didn't. That helped. That we aren't really shuffling around, wearing bandages, flesh dropping from our bones also helps. That only happens in Hollywood—and when we can't get enough human brains. If you actually meet a zombie in rotted condition, he's been without proper zombie nutrition for some time and is probably near death. Real death, he will cease to exist, fade, turn to dust and no longer be among the walking dead.

This is why; contrary to popular opinion, there won't be a zombie apocalypse. We live on human brains, and if there were to be a zombie apocalypse, we would run out of food. True we can make due with any living flesh, but we cannot survive for long without the special nutrients found in human brains. To tell the truth, a zombie can actually absorb much of the nutrition he needs from a living brain without killing the host—again contrary to popular opinion.

I've been a zombie for many years, living peacefully in a small rural community. I'm actually fairly well liked and respected—a leader in my local church. Going to church every Sunday has helped me absorb the nutrients I need to stay healthy. Most people here never even notice what they lose, as most aren't that smart to begin with.

I never thought I would be interested in politics. I like my small community and as a leader in the local church, I follow the golden rule and do onto others (except for that little brain nutrient draining I do twice a week). And I work hard to set a good example. So I guess in some ways I'm a community leader also.

When our last representative died in office and the governor was looking to make a quick appointment—somehow my name got forwarded to him and I was nominated. The folks in my community lobbied and cajoled and I soon found myself headed to Washington D.C.—there to represent the people who had sustained me for many years.

I guess I was happy to pay them back, as this was only supposed to be a temporary thing until the next election. Although I was told by the party, that if I was interested in running at the next election, they would be happy to endorse me. Seems not many politicians were ever interested in representing our little community.

I told them I would think about it and packed my bags to head to Washington. I was thinking about all those brains that would be available each time Congress was called into session—after all these were supposed to be some of the smartest people in the country so should have above average brains—right.

WRONG! I walked into my first session of Congress ready to draw nutrients from the brains of my fellow representatives. What I got was over 400 particles of Zombie mush. They were all Zombies like me. There wasn't a human brain anywhere to be sensed, except in the offices.

Now I understood what had killed our last representative. He was truly a good man. One who didn't have affairs, didn't have a huge office staff. Came to Washington to do his job and represent his constituents. He had also been a Zombie and had finally died from starvation.

I realized the same thing would happen to me if I followed in his footsteps, but all those years of going to church twice a week had left me with certain beliefs—the same beliefs my constituents had sent me here to uphold.

Okay, I would probably waste some taxpayer money—and have a large staff. I had to get at least enough nutrition to survive till the end of my term. Then again, there was always the chance no one would miss a few lobbyists and actual brain matter is better and lasts longer. Maybe I would seek another term if things worked out. We would have to see.

The Cup of Life

Maurus sat on his horse and gazed down at the small stone and mud building. The building itself was very plain; there were none of the usual ornate carvings or other indications this was a shrine to a god. This group of refugees had come to Britannia from Iudaea several years ago spreading their stories of a man called Christ of Galilee.

It was getting late in the day and the sun was fading. He glanced at a lone tree that sat on one of the nearby hills. More a thorny bush than a tree, its branches bare against the darkening sky. He turned to his four officers and nodded. "Let's get down there," he said. "This Joseph of Arimathea will be waiting."

The Roman Governor, Paulinius, and the local High King, Arviragus, had directed the five of them to this remote area of Britannia to escort this religious leader to some ceremony in a place called Avalon. Arviragus had seemed surprised that both the Merlin and the High Priestess appeared to be accepting of this new religion and had requested Paulinius send this escort. They were here not only to "protect" this Joseph, but also to learn what might be happening on Ynys Witrn.

An older man stepped out of the small stone building as they approached the door and bowed his head slightly. "Peace be with you, Captain," he said. "I am Joseph."

Maurus looked down at the man and frowned, his cloak was ragged though clean and in his hands he held a simple clay cup. The air of poverty seemed to be in direct conflict with the idea this man was supposed to be a religious leader. "May the gods protect you," Maurus finally said. "We are to be your escorts this evening." He paused and looked around for anyone else who might be nearby. "If you are ready."

Joseph shook his head slightly. "It will be a few more minutes, Captain. We must wait for one of the priestesses from Avalon to join us." The older man smiled. "I'm afraid you will need to leave your horses here. They will not be able to travel the path we must take." He raised his right hand and two young men stepped out of the building. "They will be properly cared for while we are gone," Joseph said.

Maurus glanced back at the others with him and nodded before he dismounted. "If you will let us know when you are ready," Maurus said. He moved away from the building, his officers following him.

"What do any of you know about this so-called new religion?" He spoke in a low voice.

"It is named for a Galilean who was crucified by Procurator Pontius Pilate approximately thirty years ago," Thracius said.

"I remember hearing about that," Vitus said. "He managed to get the local government mad at him for questioning their interpretations of their religion."

Maurus glanced at the two older members of the group. Both Thracius and Vitus' had older brothers who had served in Iudaea, and he valued their opinions. "So he was challenging the local government?"

Thracius and Vitus both looked at each other before turning back to Maurus and nodding.

"And, Paulinius allowed Arviragus to give these *Christians* twelve hides of land," Maurus said as he shook his head.

"Captain," Joseph called.

Maurus turned to see a young woman in white robes standing next to Joseph. "Let's go," Maurus said to his officers.

The young woman only nodded as they approached then motioned for them to follow her as she walked away from the small building. Maurus followed behind Joseph with his officers. He frowned as the priestess stopped, raised her arms over her head and a chill fog surrounded them. The woman turned back toward the building they had left then brought her arms down sharply. The fog cleared a bit and Maurus stared at the open area before them. A large mound with a stone slab covering it was where the building had been. A body was laid out on the stone.

"You are expected," the woman said motioning toward a small group of robed figures standing near the stone. She turned and stepped back into the remaining mists then vanished.

"Witchcraft," Quintus said.

"The power of their goddess," Joseph said. "Captain, you and your men must wait here during the ceremony."

"Maurus," Thracius said looking at a nearby hill. "Doesn't that look like the same tree?"

"It can't be the same tree," Laurentius said.

"How many trees are that bare at the spring equinox?"

Maurus looked at the tree with its bare branches now only shadows against the darkening sky. "We only walked a few passus from the building before the fog surrounded us. We then turned back and the fog faded. We never left Ynys Witrn. It is the same tree." He turned his attention to the group around the stone then gestured for the others to watch the area.

Joseph stood at the head of the stone, the cup he had brought held before him. Two of the robed figures moved to stand on either side of the stone, near the head. Maurus felt his eyes widen as one of the figures pushed the cowl of their robe back to reveal long, dark hair. The air stirred for a brief moment and the robe showed clearly the person standing there was a woman.

"Eithne, the High priestess of Avalon," Laurentius said. "The one across from her carries the staff of The Merlin, but he is too young to be Talfryn."

Maurus turned to look at the young man. "You seem to know something of the religion of this place."

"I was born here, Captain," Laurentius said. "My mother has a sister who serves as a priestess in Avalon, though she herself no longer observes the rituals."

Maurus nodded and turned his attention back to the ceremony the others were performing.

Joseph began speaking. "As one who recently came among you, the Lady Eithne has asked that I preside over this ceremony. Are there any here who object?"

Silence greeted Joseph's question as he waited for several seconds. "Let it be known that Talfryn, once Merlin of Breton has been called by the Dragon and has passed beyond the veil. Today we anoint Peregrin as the one now called to serve as The Merlin."

He placed the cup he was holding on the stone then Eithne removed a sword from under her robes and laid it next to the cup. The man across from the priestess held up a crystal that glowed yellow in the light of the full moon then set it with the other two objects.

"Before we can recognize The Merlin, we first bid farewell to Talfryn," Joseph said. "May his spirit find rest with the Dragon even as his body is returned to the land of which it is a part."

A blue mist flowed from the cup and swirled around the sword and crystal before it covered the body on the stone. The blue shroud lay over the body and when it faded, the body was also gone.

"The Cup of Christ, the Sword of the Goddess and the Tear of the Dragon," Laurentius said. "Three relics of these religions. That explains why Arviragus wanted us here."

"How so?" Maurus continued to watch the ceremony as Joseph picked up the cup then poured a few drops from a water skin into it.

"He cares not for this Joseph, only that Eithne returns the sword Excalibur."

The priest, as Maurus was beginning to think of this Joseph of Arimathea, then dipped his fingers into the cup and brought them up to Peregrin's lips and touched them. "The Dragon has called and you have answered, Merlin of Breton," Joseph said.

Peregrin bowed his head slightly then picked up the stone Laurentius had called the Tear of the Dragon.

Eithne reached for the sword and held it pointed at the new Merlin. "You are bound to the land and the people," she said. "Do you accept that bond and the responsibility that comes with it? The duty to protect and guide the people? To care for the land and all that dwell therein?"

Peregrin didn't say anything as he reached out and grasped the blade of the sword in his left hand then pulled his hand slowly back, still holding the blade. Blood dripped from his hand and onto the stone.

"The Goddess has accepted your oath," Eithne said as she lowered the sword.

"Lady Eithne," Joseph said. "Will you also accept the blessing from the Cup?"

"In that you have honored our beliefs and have sought to learn as well; I too would honor yours."

Joseph again dipped his fingers into the cup then touched the High Priestess's lips.

"It will be interesting to see what effects this will have," Laurentius said.

Maurus spun around and stared at the younger man. "Explain."

"Those who follow this new religion claim the cup belonged to this Christ of Galilee and that Joseph of Arimathea used it to catch his blood when his side was pierced by a spear at his crucifixion. The legends also say this Christ of Galilee again walked among the living three days after his burial. Supposedly when Joseph of Arimathea told this news to the Sanhedrin they had him imprisoned in a tomb for a score of days. The only thing he carried with him was that cup. When the tomb was opened, he was still alive. It is believed it was the cup which sustained him."

"And does your mother have a sister who follows this religion?" Maurus glared at Laurentius.

"Uh, no Sir."

"That new girl he has been seeing," Vitus said, "has been visiting the place where some of this religion's followers meet in Londinium."

"Would that be the blonde or the red-head?" Maurus grinned at Laurentius.

"Caron has brown hair."

"Guess I'm a couple of girls behind." Maurus glanced back at Joseph and the others. The group of seven was still talking though it appeared the ceremony itself was over. He motioned for his other two officers to join him.

"You said it would be interesting to see what effect the use of the cup to bless the Merlin and this priestess had. Based on the legends you told me about this cup are you saying you expect it to grant them extended life or something?" Maurus asked.

"That is doubtful as they did not actually drink from the cup. One of the ceremonies practiced by those who follow this Christ of Galilee is the sharing of bread and wine. Bread and wine, which they claim symbolize his body and blood and which they believe will grant them eternal life after death," Laurentius said. "But, that was not what I speaking of. The fact the Lady of the Lake and the Merlin both are willing to accept this blessing shows they fear this new religion will start to supplant the old ways. They are seeking to find a way to draw it into their power. With the stories told of

Christ's death and resurrection, it is possible the priestesses of Avalon only view him as another incarnation of the Horned God. One to be sacrificed as necessary while their goddess still reigns. From what Caron has told me, these followers of Christ recognize only one god and view all others as false."

"Captain." Thracius nodded at the group now walking toward them.

"Captain Maurus," Joseph said. "The ceremony is complete and we will be returning to the Chapel. I also have a request to make."

Maurus nodded then waited for the priest to continue.

"Peregrin, Eithne and I are to travel to Londinium so the Sword of the Goddess can be returned to the High King. Peregrin will also be presented as the new Merlin. We ask that you and your officers accompany us."

"Very well."

Maurus waited as Eithne raised her arms and the fog again surrounded them. When she lowered her arms and the fog faded they found themselves back on Ynys Witrn looking at the small chapel.

~ * ~

Maurus sat on his horse and looked down at the small chapel. Most of Joseph's followers had left Ynys Witrn to travel to various areas around Britannia in preparation for celebrations to commemorate the birth of their Christ of Galilee. During the time he and his officers had escorted Joseph, Eithne and The Merlin to Londinium and back to Ynys Witrn he had heard Joseph retell the story of how the cup had kept him alive. Even the High Priestess and Merlin seemed to believe the story. And if the story were true then perhaps there was something to the idea the cup could also grant eternal life to one who drank from it.

~ * ~

Word had finally come to Governor Paulinius about the burning of Rome and the hand the Christians there had in it. Both Paulinius and Arviragus had been bothered by the news and even more so now that this group seemed to be gaining new converts here in Britannia. Maurus offered to destroy the chapel, steal the cup they claimed belonged to Christ, and then take it to Rome to present to the Emperor as a prize.

"Let's go," Maurus said as he tapped his horse with his heels.

The small building was quiet as the five soldiers entered. Maurus glanced at the candles set in the wall niches, their dancing flames casting weak shadows in the room. Three wooden benches sat in front of a small table. In the center of this table sat the cup he had seen Joseph use to give his blessing to The Merlin and the High Priestess of Avalon. There were no guards in the room with the object, nor was there anything separating the table from the rest of the room. As he walked up to the table, he looked up at the statue of a woman behind the table. The only window in the room was above the statue and the light seemed to create an aura around the woman. She was holding a baby in her arms as she gazed down at the benches in the room.

"The Virgin Mary," a voice said nearby. "She is the mother of Christ and sister to Joseph."

Maurus turned to see a young man standing in an archway to his right. "I thought all of the priests were traveling at this time," he said.

"Most are." The young man stepped forward and nodded his head slightly. "I am Cathen, and I was given the duty to care for the chapel until the others return. Is there some way I can assist you, Captain?"

Maurus drew his sword and thrust it into the young man's chest. "For what your kind did to Rome, you can die," he said. Maurus picked up the cup. "Burn it," he ordered as he walked out of the building.

Maurus and his officers stood and watched as the flames surrounded the small building. He doubted the fire would last very long as there wasn't much to burn, but it still gave him some satisfaction.

"There is supposed to be a natural spring nearby," Thracius said as the flames started to die down.

"The idea of immortality appeals to you," Maurus said. He looked around at the others.

"Just as it does to you, Captain."

It didn't take the five of them long to locate the spring. Maurus filled the cup and swirled the water in it for a minute as the light from the setting sun hit the clay and seemed to color the water red. He raised the cup in salute before he took a long drink.

"By all the gods!" Maurus cursed and spit the water out as he flung the cup into the spring. "Blood. It's blood." Water from the spring splashed as the cup hit it and sank from sight.

The water from the spring rose and covered the four officers in a shower of blood. Maurus' hand went to his sword as the other four fell to the ground writhing and screaming. "By all the gods." His voice was harsh and he took several steps back as a fog covered the bodies of his officers. "Laurentius. Thracius. Vitus. Quintus." He called their names over and over as he stood there unable to see through the thick fog. The screams turned to howls as the fog began fading.

He drew his sword as the fog vanished and four large wolves stood before him. "What? Laurentius?" One of the wolves took a hesitant step forward and cocked its head to the side as it looked up at him. "Thracius? Vitus? Quintus?" Each time he called one of their names one of the wolves moved forward as if he were answering to the name.

Maurus dropped his sword and sat on the ground staring at the spring whose waters now ran blood red. He felt his stomach tighten as he continued to watch the water. "Blood," he whispered. He dipped his hand into the spring and looked at the liquid cupped in his palm. Without hesitation he brought his hand up his lips and swallowed the thick, warm fluid.

~ * ~

"My Lord," the old man said bowing. "This is the forth attack in as many days. We have lost half of our sheep and last night two of the children were killed."

"And why were your children out where wolves could attack them after dark?"

"My Lord, the children were not out of the house; they were found dead in their beds. It was as if all of the blood had been drained from their bodies."

"Where there any marks on the bodies?"

"Only two puncture marks on their necks. No other marks."

"Burn the bodies."

"My Lord?"

"You heard me, burn the bodies. They have been cursed and the curse will spread if you do not do as I command." He kicked his horse and galloped past the old man. When he reached the wooded area outside of the village, four more riders joined him.

"We must move on," Laurentius said. "They will soon begin hunting for us since you killed the children."

Maurus nodded. He had wanted to stay on Ynys Witrn, near the spring that ran as blood, but the priests had returned and began rebuilding their chapel. Their presence and the presence of their god's holy symbols had caused him and his officers pain; they had been unable to stay. So they left the isle and began traveling through Britannia. After their transformation that first night, the other four now only seemed to change into wolves during the three nights when the moon was its fullest. Even in their animal forms they remained loyal to him.

For himself, he found he now craved blood on a regular basis. Normal food would not quench his hunger and did not seem to provide him with nourishment and the blood of animals only seemed to heighten his need.

He didn't know if this was a punishment from the Christian god for killing the priest and stealing the cup or if it was one being visited on him by his own gods for allowing himself to believe in the legends told by those who followed a Galilean who was crucified for treason against the state.

It didn't matter. He had gained his immortality, but at a price. A very steep price.

Wolves of the Comancheria

Star Wolf, our shaman named me Wolf Shadow in my naming ceremony. My parents would not have held the ceremony, except he insisted—saying he had read the signs and I would be a great warrior. The only problem with this was that I was a girl. Girls were not raised to be warriors among the N*mᴜmᴜ*. However, he was the shaman—the only person in our clan whose voice carried more authority was the chief. After Star Wolf came the most respected of the warriors—my father—Stalking Wolf—who knew to argue with the Shaman would cause him to lose honor within the clan and his position as war leader. So he did as he was told and stood there as Star Wolf lifted me in his hands, presenting me to the spirits and naming me Wolf Shadow and proclaiming I would be a warrior.

The wolf was our totem, which was why every shaman carried the name Star Wolf. No child, other than the one destined to become the Shaman, was ever given a wolf name in their naming ceremony. To be named after the clan totem was an honor that had to be earned. Yet, here I was, a girl child, a new born babe—and I was to be given a wolf name in my naming ceremony and I was destined to be a warrior.

The winds swirled around my small body and the winter air grew even colder as several clouds blinded the moon from watching, what many in the clan thought to be heresy. Comanche women were strong and our enemies knew to attack our camps, even if the warriors were not there, was folly. But they were not recognized warriors as I had been named. Even as the clouds covered the moon's face, the stars remained bright. The brightest was the wolf star—the star of the shaman and of our clan.

~ * ~

When I was old enough to begin toddling after my mother, she took my hand and led me over to my father. "She may be only a girl child, but she was named a warrior by Star Wolf. She is your

123

responsibility now. My father just glared down at me then nodded. He picked me up and carried me outside then whistled sharply. His horse, a tri-colored stallion trotted up and snorted.

"First lesson, ride." He put me on the horse, stepped back and slapped the horse on the back.

I grabbed for the mane and held as tight as I could. It wasn't enough. I came off the horse and fell to the ground. My head struck a rock and the last thing I remember was my father laughing.

~ * ~

I woke to find myself on a vast plain. I was no longer a child, but a woman grown and standing in front of me was a shadowy, spirit horse. A pack of spectral wolves surrounded both of us.

"Wolf Shadow, you were named and the wolf's shadow you will be."

I continued to stare at the horse, not understanding what was meant.

A silver fog surrounded me concealing the spirits and when it cleared, I was still on the ground, my father no longer laughing. Standing over me was a black horse with a shimmering gold mane and tail. The horse lowered his head and snorted softly in my face, then tapped me gently with his hoof urging me to get up. With some effort I pulled myself up and stood next to the horse. I patted the horse on the neck then stopped as I realized I was still in the body I had worn in the spirit world. No longer a young child, but a woman grown.

"The spirits have called Wolf Shadow to follow the path they have laid out for her," Star Wolf said. I turned toward him and took a step back against the black horse. Star Wolf was kneeling next to the body of my child self. He looked up, turned toward me and nodded. "Let her be honored as the warrior she will be."

"She is a child—not a warrior," my father said. "She has earned no honors." He took a step toward Star Wolf. "Let her be buried accordingly."

The black bumped me with his nose and I climbed on his back. Let them argue about the disposition of my previous body, it would not matter. My spirit would not seek vengeance even if proper honors were not made.

~ * ~

The horse carried me north toward whatever destiny awaited. I don't how many days we traveled, hunger wasn't a concern for either of us and the horse never tired—maintaining a steady pace throughout the hours as the sun rose and set. When he finally stopped, we were overlooking a small valley in the Wichita's. The land was shrouded in mist as the moon rose full and bright. I slid off my horse and waited for a sign this was where I needed to be. From out of the mist a pack of wolves loped toward the two of us. I stood there, with no weapons, and waited as the alpha male separated himself from the others and came up to me.

"You are Wolf Shadow," a voice said. "These are your shadows."

I looked down at the alpha wolf who looked back up, his gaze not wavering for several heartbeats before he finally lowered his head. I only nodded my acceptance of his submission—this was not a dog to be patted and praised. This was a wolf, a predator, one that had acknowledged me as his alpha and to whom I could show no weakness.

"This valley was once home for a small clan of the Numunu. until they were betrayed by their kin. Now, those who would betray others are punished by the spirits of those who were betrayed."

The mist parted and I watched as a group of specters rose from the ground. They turned toward me and raised their weapons in salute. Now, I understood what was required. I would be the Wolf Shadow who sent those condemned as betrayers to their punishment.

~ * ~

I sat on Midnight Sun and waited for the group of white travelers to make their camp for the night. Three of the men in this group had been part of the group who murdered Indian Agent Neighbors. A murder ignored by the other members of the white community just as murders of Numunu by whites went unpunished and were even praised. Neighbors was an honorable man who honestly tried to help the Numunu and the whites find a way to live peaceably together. For his efforts he had been murdered. Now, the last three men involved in that murder would finally be sent to their punishment.

The wolf pack howled and I smiled at the scent of fear that came from the camp. The air cooled as the moon rose in the sky. The wolf star shone brightly as I gave a screech owl call three times and was answered by a short yip from the pack alpha. I tapped Midnight Sun lightly with my heels and he galloped toward the camp. In the silence of the night, his hooves rang and echoed—a staccato beat similar to the beat of a heart. The wind whistled around us and I knew all anyone who might be awake would see was a shadowy figure on a black horse. A specter in the night—nothing more. None would see the results until the morning as none but the ones targeted would awaken.

With care I aimed my bow—each arrow striking only the man it was meant for. Behind me, the growls of the pack grew and joined the screams of the men as the wolves tore them to pieces. In the morning, the rest of the camp would awaken to find the men's bedrolls shredded and their mangled carcasses—a warning to any who had knowledge of their crimes. The *Nᵤmᵤnᵤ* arrows would also be a warning. That no one else was killed would be considered a blessing. That no one had been awakened in the night during the massacre would be enough to convince others it had been something other than mortal men who had committed the act.

With the next full moon these men would find themselves in a small valley in the Wichita's; a place where they would find their punishment and the spirit of a white man who respected the *Nᵤmᵤnᵤ* and the other peoples of the Comanchería would be able to find justice for his murder.

~ * ~

Quanah looked at the map. The lands of the Comanchería had been taken from them. They were no longer allowed to hunt in the lands where they had lived, roamed and fought for many generations. They were warriors no more. Instead, they were supposed to be farmers, ranchers, a defeated people in a land not their own. They had been betrayed by another band of the People, ones who had sold their skills to the invaders for the same empty promises the whites had given to the People since they had first met. Promises that would be broken just as they always were. The

Penatɯka had betrayed their kin, thinking the whites would allow them to continue to roam freely in the Comanchería.

There were many who didn't believe the People had any strong spiritual beliefs. True they had few rituals and ceremonies that others knew about, but they knew true ties to the spirits came from within not from a ritual. And while many of the People would ride forever with honor and glory in the afterlife, there was also a special place reserved for those who betrayed their kin. Something the *Penatɯka* would learn in the afterlife and possibly in this life.

A Game of Marbles

Jania removed the package from the message slot and looked at it. A thick brown envelope, it had a squishy feel that told her it was padded to protect the contents. Other than her delivery code there was nothing on the front of the package. She slowly turned it over, almost dropping it when she saw the golden vortex seal covering the flap. It was from the tournament organizer. Her hands shook as she opened the seal. Inside was a gold circle-shaped badge. She had made it. She was in this year's tournament. Jania smiled then removed the remaining materials from the envelope.

Included with the badge was a sheet outlining the rules of the contest. The restrictions on her game piece as well as a copy of the board layout with the rotational rates, orbital speeds and sizes of the other game pieces.

She laughed at the extreme ego of the board's creator to actually include this information. True this was considered to be the toughest maze to compete on, but every other maze board was kept secret until the player was ready to make their attempt at navigating it.

She started to toss the layout into the recycle slot then paused as she looked at it again. Very few players were ever invited to attempt navigating this maze, and only a tiny portion of those ever succeeded. If she wanted to maintain her undefeated record, she might want to take advantage of anything that was given to her.

She glanced at the date on the papers—she had two weeks to prepare. She would be ready.

~ * ~

Jania carefully studied the layout of the maze board. The different sized jewels circled the larger one in the middle. It appeared so simple. Yet, she knew many others before her had attempted to navigate their individual stones through this maze.

Several had done so successfully; most failed. The ones who

accomplished this difficult feat were invited back to demonstrate their skills. She knew she would be one of those. She had studied the information in the contest package until she could recite it in her sleep.

Jania watched now as one of those successful participants placed his tiny silver marble on the maze board. Like many of the others, he would only return at certain times in the maze's cycle. For this participant it was every seventy-six cycles.

The small silver orb streaked quickly across the midnight black of the board's surface, leaving a shimmering glow in its wake as it passed the various marbles on the board. The tiny marble circled the large yellow gem in the center then exited the board.

The crowd of spectators, hidden in the shadows beyond the maze area, let out the collective breath they had been holding, then began cheering, whistling and clapping. The demonstrator picked up his silver stone from the return slot, bowed to the maze's creator and the unseen audience.

So easy, Jania thought as she applauded. *He makes it look so easy. Even with his game piece's close passage past the sixth and second stones there never appeared to be any risk of it contacting the ones on the board.*

"In addition to Haley's scheduled reappearance, we have a new challenger tonight. Jania, if you will join us at the table."

Jania held her head high and stepped out of the waiting booth.

"Are you ready?"

"I believe so," she said staring at the board.

"You know the way the maze works?"

"I do."

"You may launch when you are ready." The game master stepped away from the board with expansive wave of his hands.

Jania smiled slightly as she placed her small gray marble on the board at the designated spot and released it. She watched with satisfaction as the stone passed the four outer jewel-like orbs on the board without mishap.

As her marble passed the fifth orb, a large stone with swirling bands of red, white and other colors, she realized this one had affected her small marble much less than she anticipated. This caused her game piece to move less than she wanted it to and it intersected with the next stone on the board. Both marbles were destroyed with an explosive force leaving only a pile of rubble. The rubble tried to continue its circuit of the board until it was scattered in a circle surrounding the inner four marbles.

Jania looked up at the game master. "It appears I miscalculated the amount of force the fifth stone applied to my marble," she said.

The game master looked up and smiled. "It's okay. I think I will leave the debris there. It will create an interesting addition to the board. Perhaps you will return to try your luck another time."

~ * ~

"Daddy, where did the asteroid belt come from?" The child sat with her father as they gazed up at the stars.

"Some say it's material left over from when the planets were formed. It was just left drifting there instead of being used. I've also heard it was a planet which was destroyed; possibly by a large meteor or a comet."

"Could that happen to us?"

"It's highly doubtful, Janet." They sat in silence and studied the stars for several minutes. "Look," he said, pointing up, "there's a shooting star. Make a wish."

Eternal Escapes

Looking to escape your old life and start a new one? Then you need to visit me. Who am I? I'm Richard LaFayette and I'm the director of Eternal Escapes Funeral Home. Wait, don't panic. Yes, we offer the traditional services for those who have passed, but we also offer additional services for those who need to escape this life. After all once you're dead, who can come after you?

~ * ~

"I've managed Eternal Escapes for several years now. To the outside world, it appears to be a normal funeral home, one that has been in the LaFayette family for generations. The original building was part of a church and the long ago member of the LaFayette family, who established Eternal Escapes, had the grounds blessed not only by the priest before he left New Orleans, but also by several priests and priestesses of different local religions. There are stories handed down in the oldest journals that say the great Voodoo Priestess Marie Laveau herself had a hand in casting the magic this place uses.

"Funeral homes here in New Orleans have long faced a challenge—the water. There are places in this city where you can't bury a body in the ground because of the water table. Well, Eternal Escapes offers a different solution—internment in a different time and place."

I paused and looked at the young woman sitting across from me. She was dressed in a tattered dress, wooden shoes and her blue eyes were wide—both with fear and excitement. She had appeared in the coffin room after I returned the sarcophagus used for the Egyptian style funeral of an elderly woman who believed she was the reincarnation of some forgotten temple priestess of Bast. Her linen wrapped body was safely interred with thousands of cat bodies in the Great Tomb at the Temple of Bast. A minor mystery if anyone ever realizes there is a human body with all the cats and other predators interred there.

The girl seated across from me continued to watch me with those luminous blue-eyes. The universe had been telling me for a couple of years I would soon have to retire by bringing 'replacements' here to train—just as I had been brought here from my place in time to become part of the LaFayette family and director of this unique funeral home. There was none of the terror I had seen in the eyes of the boy who had been the last one brought here. There was fear—yes, but there was also excitement and curiosity. Good signs. Maybe my time had indeed finally come.

"What is your name?" I asked.

"Lieke."

I nodded. "Messenger."

She nodded.

"To fit into this place and time, we should change it." I held up my hand before she could protest. "I had to do the same when I was brought here Lieke. Before I became Richard, I was Sorley—which is a summer traveler in my native tongue." I hadn't thought about it before, but it had been summer when I had been brought here.

I paused for a brief moment and saw the tiny nod she gave me. I wanted to keep her name tied to her home, but wasn't sure how to translate Lieke. Then it hit me—flowers. The Nederlands was renowned for their flowers, tulips in particular, but also: "Lily," I said.

Lieke, now Lily smiled at me. "Lily LaFayette," she said. Even as she said, her speech changed slightly, adopting a delicate southern accent. Not heavy like Hollywood made them, but soft, gentle—just like a flower—just like a Lily.

I had one more thing to tell her. "Right now, you still have the option to go home. Until you actually agree to stay and become the next Director of Eternal Escapes, you are not required to stay. However, if you agree to stay you will not be able to leave until you have trained someone to take over after you. This place is a blessing for many, but it is also a trap."

~ * ~

That was almost a year ago and Lily has become an integral part of Eternal Escapes. Her caring and empathic manner always re-assures those who are struggling with making the final or 'Eternal' arrangements for a loved one. One thing I've also noticed about her is she spends most of her free time in the library room.

The library room here at Eternal Escapes is as unique as the services we offer. We have texts covering centuries of history—almost every historical period and culture is represented in our books and occasional scrolls. Some retrieved from the time period they cover. Then there are the books that cover the funeral practices of those cultures. Lily was a quick study and she worked well with the families of our clients in helping them make decisions. The only book she hadn't read yet was the 'record' book of the director. That book was created by the same magic that created Eternal Escapes. The histories it held were the histories of those who used our services to escape to a new life.

~ * ~

"Our son was killed in Iraq," the heavy set woman said.

"But you don't want a military funeral," Lily said.

"No." The man took his wife's hand and squeezed it lightly. "We disagreed with the war and we didn't want him to join the army. He was always headstrong, never listened to us and now he's gone."

I heard the bitterness in the man's voice, the pain and even the pride. These were parents who had struggled to make sure their son was strong and independent. That was something they were proud of. They just felt his death had been in vain—because they disagreed with the cause.

Lily nodded. "You want to honor his bravery, but you don't want the military involved. Am I correct?"

I was puzzled by the direction Lily was taking the conversation, but let her continue as I made notes in the ledger. Both parents nodded, and that told me she was on the correct track. I knew the Tafoya's didn't have much money and would have been reluctant to have their son interred in one of the community cemeteries where after one year and day, if you didn't pay again the body could be removed and the plot used for someone else. At least the old prohibitions on cremation were no longer in place, but even then there was still the assumption you had to pay for an expensive casket and all the extras. Too many funeral homes preyed on the grief of the families and pushed the idea you needed to send the deceased off in style. Perhaps a carry-over of ancient traditions of interning the deceased with their valuables. The Pharaohs of Egypt, the Vikings, and others. Of course, the Vikings also cremated their dead.

For a moment, I wondered if she was thinking of a Viking funeral. Those were a bit more difficult to perform properly. The city and county didn't like us launching a Viking style ship in Lake Pontchartrain and setting it on fire. Typically, for the few we had done, we cremated the body first, then used a replica Viking boat in the small pond here on the property. Most families understood. I wasn't sure that was what these parents would want for their son.

"You taught him to be strong, to stand up for himself, to fight for what he believed in, to defend others," Lily said softly.

The father nodded.

Lily looked at me. "Sparta?"

I nodded.

"Like in that movie 300?" The father asked.

"Yes. Although Hollywood took many liberties with that story—it did capture the spirit of the Spartan people as recorded in legend."

I saw a light in the mother's eyes. Yes, she liked this idea. No flag draped coffin, no twenty-one gun salute—but recognition of the reasons why he joined the military. Recognition of his service, but nothing to tie it to a war they disagreed with.

"Please understand, we don't have much, but..." The father let his voice trail off.

That was my cue. "Sir, we do understand and don't worry, this will be the final price." I handed him a slip of paper.

He handed the paper to his wife. "I don't understand," he said. "This is barely a fraction of what other funeral homes wanted."

"Sir, Eternal Escapes has been here for many years. We can afford to base our prices on what people can pay." I smiled. "One of the advantages of the specialized services we offer."

"Thank you."

"Now you understand that this will be a cremation."

They both nodded.

"There will be a memorial plaque placed in the alcove of your choice and we have several different ones you can select from," Lilly said. "I do have a few recommendations." She picked up a small book. She always seemed to have a sixth sense of what the families would want and had already narrowed the possibilities.

"Let's take a look at the alcoves." She stood and waited for the parents.

I knew the first one she would be taking them to, the Alcove of Nike—the Goddess of Victory. I also knew every one of the plaques she would recommend would also include the American flag or another service symbol. They might have disagreed with the war he was sent to, but his service was important to him. They would understand that.

I picked up my notes; I would have to see if we had a Spartan shield in the collection as well as the appropriate helmet, cloak, sword, and other items. A Spartan warrior was expected to return with his shield or on it. The pallbearers would also have to be in the appropriate attire for when they carried their comrade from the service to the crematorium.

"Hey!"

My head jerked up at my secretary's cry as a man burst into the room. In his right hand he held gun.

"Can I help you?" I stood up and held my hands away from my body.

Josephine looked at me and I gave her a slight shake of my head. She cocked her head to the side, but left the room.

"I want out. Your place has a reputation for disappearing people. I want to disappear."

"I'm sorry, but you are mistaken. This is a funeral home." I knew what he meant, but our services were meant to be used to help people who needed help. Not to assist criminals.

"Look. I know you have the power to send me somewhere else and you're going to do it." He raised the gun and pointed it at my head.

"Richard..." Lilly's voice trailed off as she entered the office.

The man jerked around and the gun dropped slightly as it fired.

"Stop." I could hear the gunman speaking even over the roaring in my ears. I was born a Viking, a warrior. But living in this time, I had not maintained my training and my reflexes were no longer sharp. Still I reached Lily and pushed her to the floor before he could bring the gun around and target her.

"Bast," I whispered as I felt my body growing cold.

"I understand." She kissed my cheek softly.

"Get up!" I felt Lily being pulled off me.

"If you don't want to end up like your boss, you'll help me vanish."

"Very well."

~*~

Lily smiled as she watched the model boat burn. She had outfitted it as richly as she could with as many Viking relics that would fit. Sorley son of Hiorvard would be received in Valhalla with the honors fitting a king and hero—as he deserved.

The setting sun painted the clouds in shades of red—adding additional flames to those already burning. Lily waited until the sun finally passed beyond the horizon and the last flame flicked out leaving only fading image of the boat.

Lily walked slowly back to the funeral home. It had been a long day. She had escorted the gunman to the coffin room and opened the standing sarcophagus. Inside was what appeared to be a tunnel leading into darkness, with a faint light at the end. The gunman hadn't even asked where it went—he just ran into the tunnel. She had no idea what he was running from, nor did she care. She just closed the sarcophagus and returned to Richard.

Her friend and mentor was already gone by the time she reached the office. With care she had prepared the body. Unfortunately, she had to cremate the body before the ceremony as the model of the ship was too small to hold Richard.

Only those who worked at Eternal Escapes attended the ceremony. All 'members' of the LaFayette family understood no one but staff was allowed to attend the services when one of the Directors retired or passed.

She paused as she entered the building. A light breeze blew across her skin and she shivered despite the warmth of the evening. There was something in the breeze, a presence, a power. She thought she heard a woman chanting softly. Lily strained to hear the words even as they faded.

The same presence or power guided her footsteps. Lily found

herself in the library. Whatever blessings enchanted the funeral home, she felt them becoming a part of her.

Eternal Escapes was anointing her as the new director.

Lily glanced around the library. Previously when Richard had guided Eternal Escapes, it had been dark wood and stone walls giving it the feel of a Viking holding.

The dark wood and stone had been replaced with a lighter wood and there was the scent of tulips in the air. It seemed larger and she couldn't tell if it was the coloring or an actual fact.

On the main desk the large black director's book sat open. She sat down and smiled. Fresh ink was drying on the pages. "You didn't get the escape you imagined."

Her blue eyes scanned the account. It recorded the gunman's journey to the Great Temple of Bast. The lovable yet unpredictable goddess once had been the protector of the Pharaoh and of Egypt.

The gunman entered my temple uninvited. He stumbled about, his clumsy feet squashing my precious ones. He thought, from the thoughts in his mind, he had escaped. This part of the tombs is sealed as it should be.

I heard the cries of my disturbed dead and awakened them. Their jeweled eyes opened and they yowled in anger.

He tried to run but their sharp claws shredded his weak human legs. He fell and my followers circled him.

Waiting.

A brave one would swat at him. Another would pounce on his back.

The human screamed, trying to push them away.

Lily suppressed a smile as she continued reading and the clear images formed in her mind. The cats interred there being reawakened by their goddess, protecting Her temple from one who would intrude and defile it.

They called to me and I came. In my cat form I could do nothing. But I had once been one even mightier.

My form melded and I rose in another form I had once held. Sehkmet, goddess of war and healing.

With a mighty roar I took pity on him and strangled him in my jaws.

He was very good eating.

~ * ~

Looking to escape your old life and start a new one? Then you need to visit me. Who am I? I'm Lily LaFayette and I'm the director of Eternal Escapes Funeral Home. Wait, don't panic. Yes, we offer the traditional services for those who have passed, but we also offer additional services for those who need to escape this life. After all once you're dead, who can come after you?

To Live

I am tired of it. Tired of the way the patriarchal religions and governments of this world have painted me over the centuries. And, it seems that with each passing century certain legends have become more ingrained than others. I have been called by many names. One of my most recognizable names is Pandora. Yep, that would be me: the first woman, given as a gift by the gods to Man, and used by those same gods to release various plagues into the world. They wanted them released, but they didn't want to lose Man's worship if he blamed them. So, they needed a scapegoat— that scapegoat was me.

Still, the time of the ancient Greeks is long past and you would think their myths would have faded in time. Oh no. After the fall of Greek civilization and the Roman Empire, who incidentally took much of their own religion from the people they conquered, came the Christians. Christianity, which also borrowed from the mythologies of others—primarily so they could find ways to claim the elder religious festivals for their own and thereby make integration of those who followed a different faith easier. They take their creation stories from the Hebrews, although they fail to acknowledge Lilith as the first woman—created from the Earth as Adam was, but who did not stay with Adam and found her own way in the world. Why they do not recognize Lilith, is beyond me. I can only assume it is because they decided Woman should be subservient to Man; just ask Paul, and didn't want to admit the first woman created by God wasn't.

After Lilith left the garden, god created me—Eve. You know the story as it is presented in the Torah and the Bible. Adam was placed into a deep sleep and God took a rib from his side and created me. This is also seen by many as another sign Woman was meant to be subservient to Man. However, there are also those who say that by taking a rib from Adam's side, God was saying we were to stand side by side as equals. Honestly, I doubt God thought about it since he had to know man would put his own interpretation on things. After all, he did give us free will didn't he?

Anyway, enough of the preaching—it is a bad habit I have when I get on my soapbox. Instead, let me tell you my story regarding how Man was thrown out of Paradise, and how it really isn't my fault.

~ * ~

My earliest memories where of standing in a beautiful garden, flowering trees and plants created an explosion of color and scent. I knew the names of all of these plants as well as the names of all the animals I saw as I stood there. All of this was a part of my memory as if I had been the one to give them names. I guess in a way I had. I was Woman—meaning From Man. I stood there and looked around as several of the animals came up to me and touched their noses to my hand. After a few minutes, they turned and returned to the shelter of the trees. That was when I saw him—Adam. I already knew his name; knew we a part of each other. But, beyond that, there was nothing.

He looked at me and smiled.

"Adam this is Eve," another voice said. "She is to be help-meet and companion to you."

I smiled as God appeared next to me and took my hand then reached for Adam's and joined our hands together. I knew who God was and accepted his statement that Adam and I were to be companions. However, you will notice he never said I was to be Adam's property. Of course, all things considered, you have to wonder if his claims of giving Man free will really applied at this point.

Life was pleasant for us in that garden. We were like young children who had the most marvelous playground in the world to play in. When Man looks back at the legends and decides they need to blame someone for the ills they now suffer, they always seem to forget that they would never have existed if Adam and I had never left the garden. We would have been like children forever—never growing old—forever innocent; living under the protection of our father.

But, like all children, we eventually had to leave our parent's house and there was still that annoying rule about free will God wanted in place. Children may have free will in some things, but they are still bound to the rules of their parents.

Now, for Adam and I, there really were no rules, other than we were not to eat the fruit of a particular tree. God called it the tree of knowledge of good and evil and then told us that if we did eat from the fruit of the tree we would die. We didn't really understand what that meant, as we had no experience with death. And, what child really understands what death is? Usually one who has been robbed of their innocence—which in and of itself is one of the greatest sins there is.

As I said, we were as children. We took pleasure in each other's company, just being together. We stayed in the garden, not that there was anywhere else to go. While the Bible says Man was created in order to care for the land, there was nothing that needed caring for in the garden. Just as I was Adam's companion, we were also Gods companions and he visited us often. I think that was what we really were. The animals were pets—we were children, friends and companions. After all, we were made in his image.

How long were we in the garden? I honestly do not know. Time is a concept Man developed after we left. The changing of the days really has no meaning in a place where there are no seasons; where there are no places to be or things that require doing. Think back to when you were a young child—before you had to worry about school; when all you had to do was play with your friends. Did you really keep count of the days? Only once you were aware of special events such as your birthday did you start to count the days. Adam and I didn't celebrate things like birthdays, so had no reason to count the days.

God didn't visit on any schedule, and we had no reason to worry about when he was coming. He arrived and left when he felt like it.

Eventually though, came a period of time, when both Adam and I realized it had been a while since God had visited us. It actually scared us a bit. This was the first strong emotion we had felt. Yes, we understood the emotion of joy and basic love, but those were simple emotions. Now, we felt something different. Neither of us knew how long it had been since he visited—all we knew was we missed him and it frightened us that he wasn't there.

I remember we fell asleep that night, holding each other tightly. Then something else happened: Adam kissed me. I think it was an accident his lips brushed mine, but it happened and we both felt a kind of electric shock go through us. The next morning, we tried it again, but it seemed different. It was wet and uninteresting. We spent the day wandering in the garden; visiting the animals that lived there with us. The only ones we didn't see were the unicorns. I am not sure why, but not having them come up to us as they normally did made me a little sad.

This became our routine for a while, as God still did not come to visit with us. Then one day, we decided to wander separately, I still don't know why—it was something we had never done before. I found myself standing in front of the forbidden tree. It was beautiful. I know some people equate the fruit to an apple, but an apple pales in comparison. The blossoms were more delicate than those of the cherry tree and more fragrant than any flower or perfume. The fruit itself shimmered with all the colors ever imagined.

There in front of the tree stood the unicorns, their horns crossed, blocking the path. Between them was the only creature of the garden who did not have a companion—the dragon. I know, the Bible calls him a serpent, but it was the dragon. Even though he never had a female companion like the other animals, the dragon never seemed to be alone; he was always there with the other animals. The only time, I never remember seeing him was when God was with us.

"Eve," the dragon said bowing his head slightly. "You whose name means to live. I would ask you if you are truly living?"

"I don't understand," I said. "I breath, I eat, I sleep. What else is there?"

"Were you not created with free will? The ability to do what you want?"

"That is what we have been told."

"Yet, despite that free will, there are things you are forbidden from doing."

"God has forbidden us nothing except for eating from the fruit of this single tree."

"And why did God forbid you from eating from this tree?"

"He told us if we ate from the fruit of the tree of the

knowledge of good and evil we would die."

"But he created it as well as creating you. Why would he create something that would kill you?"

"That I cannot answer, but God has forbidden it and I obey him."

"You obey him? But I thought you had free will."

"I do and I choose to obey him."

"Very well." The dragon bowed his head again. "Adam is looking for you. I believe he is getting scared because he does not know where you are. The unicorns will take you to him."

I nodded my thanks, but didn't say anything.

When we found Adam, I told him everything the dragon had said to me. He again kissed me and held me tightly as we fell asleep. This time the kiss had been deliberate and the spark was again there.

The unicorns were gone in the morning. We decided not to do anything this day, hoping God would visit. I wanted to talk to him about what the dragon had said. He never came. Looking back, I now realize God was testing us and testing his idea of free will. We may have failed that test, but obviously, free will passed. In the final analysis, I also believe we passed as well. What father wants his children to love him only out of obligation or because it is part of the way they were created. They want their children to love them, because they just *do*. That is the beauty of giving Man free will. Yes, there are those who have turned their backs on God, but that makes the ones who still accept and love him and try to live as he would wish, all the more precious.

That evening, after Adam fell asleep, I found myself walking the path to the tree. Once again, the unicorns and the dragon were there.

"You came back," the dragon said.

"What is death?"

"Death is something that you will never experience while you are here. It is the cessation of life. A ceasing to exist for an individual."

"Why would I want to do something that will cause that?"

"Because it is in facing death that Man will finally learn to live."

"I don't understand."

"And that is the point of the tree." The dragon lowered his head and I could see his tail was wrapped around the tree, with the tip resting on the single branch that held a pair of the fruits. It was then I realized there were only two of the fruits on the tree. One for me and one for Adam.

"This is the tree of the knowledge of good and evil. If you eat this fruit, you will lose your innocence and will grow beyond the children you are now. You will be able to know Adam as male and female."

I felt my cheeks grow warm at that remark, though I didn't understand why, and my thoughts turned to the kiss we had shared.

"You will understand much more than you do now, having knowledge only God has at this time."

I found myself staring at the fruit.

"But there is a cost."

"We would die," I said.

"Not immediately," the dragon said. "But eventually—yes. Having responsibility—not only for yourself, but also for others. Growing old and eventually dying. These are the cost of this knowledge."

The dragon paused and I saw a tear form in the eye of the unicorn mare.

"The choice is yours Eve. Would you eat of the fruit and truly be free or do you prefer to live as you are now? Forever young, forever children, never knowing or understanding anything. There is much more you can learn and have if you eat of the fruit. God has given you free will, it is your choice."

I continued to stare at the fruit.

"Eve," I heard Adam call my name.

"I am here," I said as I reached for one of the two fruits.

"What are you doing?"

"It is my choice. I know the cost, but I would prefer to live, learn and grow than remain trapped here in this garden." I stopped, leaned forward and let my lips brush his. "And I would also like to have you with me." I handed him the fruit I had pulled from the tree and reached for the remaining one.

Adam looked at me and nodded as we both took a bite.

~ * ~

I am sure most of you know what happened next—at least the part that is recorded in the Bible. We saw we were naked, were ashamed and fashioned aprons from figs leaves. Well, there was a little bit more that happened prior to that. Suffice it to say, we did know each other as male and female first. We were still lying together when we heard God in the garden. It was because he was there that we hastily fashioned the aprons. While we weren't exactly ashamed, I think that was something that later translators put in, once some people decided sex was a bad thing. We realized God had always appeared wearing some sort of garment so we tried to emulate him.

When God finally found us, he asked us why we were hiding. Adam was the one who had to open his mouth and say we were naked. Men, they never know when to keep their mouths shut.

Then God asked him about the tree and Adam's words were those of a child caught with his hand in the cookie jar. "She made me do it." Even after eating the fruit, Adam was still acting like a child. Actually, I think he was scared: scared of disappointing God, scared of being punished and scared because, thanks to the knowledge we had gained, he now understood what death really was.

"You have made your choice and because of that choice, I must now send you from my garden," God said.

He wasn't angry in his pronouncement, but I thought I heard something in his voice—sadness and perhaps a little pride.

"It is now time for you to go out into the world. You may never return to this place, but you are my children and I will always be there for you."

The two unicorns escorted us out of the garden. They both stopped at the edge, their horns crossed, blocking the path back. I know the Bible talks of two angels with flaming swords who guarded the garden—another of Man's interpretations. It is actually only two unicorns who shed tears for the lost innocence of Man. The only two unicorns created by God, as they are the true guardians of Man's innocence and will never have to leave his garden.

Over the millennia, I have heard people say that Judas, the

betrayer of Christ, was necessary for God's plan and he truly had no choice in his actions. There is even a book claiming to be the Gospel of Judas, which much of the Christian church refuses to acknowledge, that says Christ told Judas to act as he did. So here are these people trying to defend the person who betrayed the Son of God so he was crucified on a Roman cross, yet I rarely if ever hear anyone defending my actions.

If I had not listened to the dragon, mankind would never have existed. So, despite the chauvinistic attitudes of people like Paul and others who would keep a patriarchal system in place, without me you wouldn't be here. God's command to us to be fruitful and multiple is the one that gave birth to my descendants. And unfortunately, it is also the one that causes some men to believe women are to be used as nothing more than breeding stock. Perhaps Lilith had the right idea, when she walked out of the garden on her own—perhaps not. I enjoyed my life as wife to Adam and as mother to our children. There is nothing wrong with that life as long as it is not forced. Just as there is nothing wrong with the life Lilith chose for herself.

Free will. The right to choose. That is what I gave to mankind when I chose to eat that fruit. Yes, there is pain and evil in the world, but there is also joy and good. The two are a balance, as one cannot exist without the other. This is what God knew and why he gave us the fruit. He then gave us free will and hoped we would make the choice to grow up so we could truly be what he created us to be.

Maybe one of these days, people will get over their egos and realize that we had to leave the garden. If I hadn't taken that fruit, when I did, there would have been something else that would have eventually happened. It was all a part of God's plan after all. Remember what the dragon said my name meant—To Live. God created me to be helpmeet, companion and to make sure Man would live.

Pawn's Gambit

1

Malei watched the images in her mirror as the guests began to arrive at the palace. The King had invited everyone of any position from within the kingdom and the neighboring lands, as well as the fairy council, to attend the christening of his first-born child. That is; everyone but her. True, she had been exiled to this remote castle in the high mountains after she had argued against the King's coronation in favor of herself as the older sibling and had failed. But she was still his sister and she held the same power as the members of the fairy council and should have been included. However, that did not matter. She had planned for this day for several years.

She concentrated for a moment on the Queen's image, frowning at the paleness of the woman's skin and the lines still etched in her face. The princess had been born six months ago, yet the Queen looked as if she had only risen from the birthing bed a few hours prior. Malei doubted she would ever have another child.

She continued to watch as the princess was presented to the court and they re-affirmed their loyalty to the royal family. Before the feast was brought in, the members of the fairy council appeared. This was what she had been waiting for. She leaned closer to the mirror then passed her hand over it. The images sharpened and she could hear each of the fairies as they approached the baby.

"My gift to the child will be the gift of beauty. Even the dawn, for which she is named, will pale by comparison," the first said.

"And my gift is that of music," the second said. "The birds will fall silent at the sound of her voice."

Malei shook her head as the rest continued in the same vein. *Beauty, music, grace? What do these have to do with the ruling of a kingdom? They should be gifting her with things like strength, wisdom and compassion.*

She waited until the next to last of the council approached, then dropped a handful of blue powder on the floor in front of her.

~ * ~

She bowed her head slightly as she appeared in the hall amid a cloud of billowing blue smoke. "Your Majesties, it appears I must apologize for the lateness of my arrival," she said stepping forward.

"I do not believe you were actually invited," the King said.

"So, now you refuse to acknowledge the blood kinship I share with the princess and would not allow me to offer her a christening gift."

The Queen placed a shaking hand on the King's arm. "We are the ones who should apologize for the insult. And we will not stand in the way of your sister bestowing a gift on your daughter."

Malei raised an eyebrow as she bowed to the Queen. The woman had more strength than she had given her credit for. She stepped forward and looked down at the sleeping child. *So small and innocent,* she thought. For just a heartbeat, she hesitated before raising the staff she carried with her.

"The princess has been blessed by the members of the fairy council with gifts of beauty, grace, and music. These gifts will be indeed blossom as she grows. However, before the final setting of the sun of her sixteenth year, the princess shall prick her finger on the spindle of a spinning wheel and die." She dropped another handful of the powder on the floor and left the hall.

~ * ~

Back in her office, she watched the last of the fairy council approach the child, her head held high as she smiled at the King and Queen. "Fear not, your Majesties," she said. "While I cannot undo the curse, perhaps it can be modified."

Malei smiled. This was why her arrival had had to be timed properly. She knew the others would think to interfere and if several them had yet to bestow their gifts on the princess they could have combined their power and undone her spell. If she had waited till they were all done, they would have been able to use their magic to shield the princess until the last day the curse would be in effect and prevent it from happening. Now, the laws of magic bound them; they could interfere at this time or wait to see if they could prevent the final outcome of the curse. She had judged them correctly; they would interfere now, attempting to modify the curse, and she would have sixteen years to complete her plan.

"This is my gift to the princess," the last of the council said. "When she pricks her finger, she will not die. Instead she will fall into a deep sleep, one that will last until she is awakened by a brave and true prince."

"A brave and true prince?" Malei shook her head again. Another complication and one she would have to be prepared for as well. There were too many fools who thought of themselves as brave and true princes, and who would be eager to be the one to awaken the sleeping princess and thereby break the curse.

2

Malei looked up as the guards escorted the rain soaked figure into her office. The girl appeared to be no more than fourteen years old, despite this being her sixteenth birthday. Her honey blonde hair and clothes clung to her like second skins. Her black eyes stared straight ahead, not wavering as Malei's own met them.

"Why are you here?" Malei watched the girl as she snapped the question at her.

The girl blinked once, slowly, before answering.

"My family was murdered and I want vengeance."

Malei raised an eyebrow. "Are you accusing me of this act?"

"No!" the girl said quickly. "I...I want to be trained."

Malei noted the girl's hesitation. She did suspect her of being responsible for the deaths of her family. Perhaps, she still had a faint recollection of Malei's role in bringing her here.

Malei stood up and walked around the girl studying the small, lithe figure. The girl was shivering in her wet clothing. Despite her appearance, there was something about her spirit that appealed to Malei. It was stronger than she suspected it would be when she had initiated this series of events almost sixteen years ago. Maybe she had misjudged the impact the other gifts would have on this girl's life.

There was a flash of silver at the girl's throat. Malei reached out and lifted the small alicorn pendant. A tie to the life the girl had left behind. Something else she would have to take away. The girl started to grab for the pendant and Malei slapped her with her free hand. "You come to my house, asking to be trained. Do not presume to lift your hand to me!"

"As you wish," the girl said.

Malei jerked the pendant, breaking the slender chain holding it. "As I command! If you are to remain here, you will learn respect for those over you. And while you are in training, everyone is over you."

"Yes, My Lady." The girl nodded slightly.

"That is better." Malei turned and placed the girl's necklace on her desk, then picked up an egg-sized purple stone. She held the stone at the girl's eye-level, then rubbed her thumb across the top of it. A brilliant purple light burst from the stone and captured the girl's attention. Malei lowered the stone as the dark obsidian of the girl's eyes faded to clear lavender.

"For now, until you are instructed otherwise, your name is Pawn. A Pawn is all you are and all you will be, until you earn a higher place. Do you understand?"

"I understand."

Malei nodded to the guards. "Escort her to her quarters. See she is fed, given new clothes and the opportunity to bathe."

The guards bowed and led the girl from the room.

Malei sat at her desk, picked up the small pendant and caressed the winged unicorn. She carefully coiled the chain around the pendant, and then placed it on the shelf next to the purple stone before turning back to look at the door. She had waited sixteen years for this day to come.

3

Malei listened to the reports of the trainers each day and personally supervised much of the girl's training. Pawn quickly learned to use a rapier and other small bladed weapons, in both defense and attack. Her grasp of strategy and tactics was surprising in one who had been taught her primary talents were her music and beauty. Malei shook her head as she thought about that.

This girl's family only expected her to make a good marriage, just as Malei's had once expected of her.

The girl's training progressed rapidly. She was intelligent and an eager learner. She demonstrated a willingness to accept the authority of those over her. But while she was never abusive when granted authority over others, she seemed hesitant to wield that authority. That was something Malei worried about. The girl had shown strength and spirit when she first came to her citadel, but Malei now wondered if that spirit had been crushed by the months of training. If it had, all her planning would have been for nothing.

Malei walked into the dimly lit training hall. Pawn had been given a day to herself and she wanted to see how the girl was passing it. The training ring was covered in shadows as two figures sparred in the center. The ringing of the blades echoed off the stone walls as the metal flashed in the flickering torchlight.

Malei watched as Pawn sparred with one of the guards. The girl had matured well in her time here, but still carried herself with the poise and grace of her former life. Pawn's beauty and intelligence, if combined with a strong will and sense of self would make her a powerful person when her training was complete. Tomorrow would be the test to see if that time had come. If the girl's spirit had been broken she would have to hope the other half of her plan worked better than this one had.

4

Malei smiled as Pawn was escorted into the throne room of the castle. Her pale blue gown shimmered as she walked and the silver and sapphire crown sparkled brightly. The only thing missing was the silver alicorn pendant. That part of Pawn's past would only be returned when her training was completed. Another glint of silver caught Malei's eye and she nodded to herself at the small dagger Pawn was wearing under her sleeve.

"This will be a role-play scenario. You are the new Queen of this Kingdom and Pyrin is your Prince Consort. A petitioner has approached you both regarding an idea he has." Malei bowed slightly as she backed away from the throne. She stood in the shadows and watched carefully. Pawn had been given instruction in government and royal hierarchies as part of her training. She would know that as Prince Consort, Pyrin's position should be considered subservient to her own. Malei wanted to see if and how the girl would exercise her authority when Pyrin tried to usurp it in this little scene—just as her father had done to her mother.

Pawn seated herself on the throne and blushed slightly as Pyrin laid his hand on top of hers. He left his hand there as the petitioner was escorted in.

"Your Majesties," he said bowing deeply.

The man kept his attention focused on Pyrin instead of Pawn. Pawn sat quietly, smiling softly and occasionally glancing at the Prince-Consort as the petitioner explained a plan to send tutors to each of the towns and villages in the kingdom to teach the peasants to read and write. She continued to sit there without saying anything when Pyrin stood and dismissed the petitioner, saying they would consider his proposal and announce a decision within the next few days.

After the door had shut, Pawn stood and faced Pyrin, her hands crossed together lightly. "What did you think of his proposal?"

"I don't like it. Educating the peasants cannot be a good idea. It will encourage them to rise above their stations." He stood also and reached out to take her hands in his. "However, this is not a matter you need worry about, my dear. I will send a message to the man and let him know we have given the proposal its due consideration and have decided against it." He lifted her hands to his lips and kissed them.

"And what gives you the authority to do that?" Pawn pulled her hands away from Pyrin and placed them on her hips, her head cocked to the side. "You are only my consort; I am the Queen."

"My Lady, you have much more important concerns that demand your attention: the running of the castle as well as providing the Kingdom with an heir."

"The Kingdom is my primary concern and I will make the decision regarding the proposal that has been brought to us. I appreciate your opinion and I will be speaking to the council of advisers as well. This is not a decision to be made lightly."

Malei was pleased. Pawn had not made a scene regarding the petitioner's apparent dismissal of her, yet she did not back down to Pyrin when he tried to assume her authority. She had demonstrated both diplomacy and wisdom in her handling of the situation. Malei wondered what the young woman's decision regarding the proposal would be. Her father had agreed with the petitioner. Though he had not mandated that everyone would be taught to read and write, he had decreed schools would be set up and open to all. She would have to ask the girl what her opinion of the petition was. But that could wait until after the final test.

"Pawn!" Malei called. "I have an assignment for you. Change your clothes, get your weapons and report to my office."

The girl nodded then hurried out of the room.

~ * ~

Malei looked up at the girl as she entered the office. She was dressed in her leathers and carried herself with confidence. Her back was straight and her head held high as she nodded politely. This would be the last time she addressed her only as Pawn. After today, she would be a different person. The girl she had been when the original spell had been triggered was dead, and a new person had been forged in her place.

"When you came here you said you wanted revenge for the murder of your family. The time has come for you to achieve it. This man," Malei passed her hand over the mirror on her desk, "is the one responsible for the deaths of your family. I can send you to his castle. My magic will return you here once you have accomplished your assignment."

The girl looked at the image in the mirror and tightened her hand on the dagger at her side. "I understand," she said.

Malei tossed a handful of the blue powder on the floor in front of Pawn and watched the girl vanish in a swirl of smoke. Then she passed her hand over the mirror on her desk. The polished silver clouded for a moment to show the girl standing in the shadows of a long hallway. Dust covered the floor and spider webs hung from the burned out torches and empty sconces. Pawn didn't seem to notice the signs of neglect as she moved through the corridors, but the girl's soft leather boots left almost no trace of her passing.

Malei touched a corner of the mirror and the scene changed slightly. Now, she could see what the girl was seeing.

~ * ~

Pawn pressed back into a curtained alcove as footsteps approached from an adjoining hallway. Malei had shown her an image of the man who had ordered her family's death, but she had not told her specifically where to find him. From the picture she assumed he was a man of some importance as he had been well dressed and wore a thin gold band on his head. If he held some type of power in this place, then it seemed reasonable he would have an audience hall. It was that location she wanted to find.

She waited until the footsteps passed her then slipped out from behind the curtain. She watched the two guards turn down another hallway before moving to follow them.

A statue stood at the corner and she found enough space to stand between it and the wall as she risked a quick glance down the other hall. There, at the end of the hallway was a set of double doors and guards stood on either side. The other two guards waited as the doors were opened and an older man stepped out of the room. The guards saluted as he walked past them. It was the same man Pawn was here for.

The guards did not accompany the man and Pawn moved from one shadowed area to another as she followed him. She was surprised to find the corridors empty except for herself and the one she was after, but she wanted to wait until they were both in a room or other less accessible place before striking. After what seemed like an hour of following the man through the corridors of the castle, he opened a door and stepped into a room.

She waited for several minutes to see if he exited or if any voices could be heard in the silence of the hallway. Only the creak of a chair as someone might have sat down reached her. She moved to the door, which had been left ajar. The man was sitting in a large cushioned chair, his back to the door, as he appeared to be looking out a window.

She slipped past the door and into the room. She caught her breath at the sound the metal of the dagger made as she pulled it from the sheath. The man in the chair didn't react in any way and she offered a silent thank you to whichever power was watching over her.

The man turned and looked up as she approached the chair. "Why are you here?" His voice was soft as he spoke.

"To take payment for the death of my family." She shoved the blade into his chest. The strike was perfect, passing just under the breastbone and into his heart

She stared at the man for a moment as he slumped in the chair. There had been no protest, no struggle, no attempt to call for help. He had let her kill him. It made no sense to her. Her hand shook as she removed the blade from the body and stared at the blood on the now dull metal. A chill wrapped itself around her and she closed her eyes for a moment. When she opened them the scene had changed. The man was still there, blood staining his clothes, but everything else was covered in dust—the dust of many years.

She looked again at the man she had killed. She knew this person. The golden band he wore on his graying hair and the slender hands that rested in his lap. A glint of silver sparkled at his neck and she reached out with a trembling hand. He wore an alicorn pendant. She snatched her hand back, but continued to stare at the pendant as it rested against the dark blue of the man's clothes. Her hand went to her own throat for a moment as her vision blurred with a lavender haze. When the haze faded, she glanced at the body in the chair again.

"Father?"

Pawn dropped the dagger, the metal of the blade ringing as it hit the stone floor. She felt her heart pounding—her whole body drumming with the rhythm as she tried to catch her breath.

"Malei!" She finally forced the name out between breaths as she picked up the dagger.

Now she realized exactly who it was she had gone to. There had been no attack against her family. She had met an old woman who had offered to show her how to spin thread. When she took the spindle, she had pricked her finger. The next thing she remembered she had been standing outside the gates to Malei's castle in the high mountains.

Malei. The name came back to her memory as the stories she had been told in her childhood resurfaced. She was a witch who had tried to overthrow her father. The fairy council had supported him and it was their power which had exiled her to the mountains. Pawn also remembered hearing rumors that the witch had appeared at her christening and had attempted to place some sort of curse on her—one the fairy council had been able to counter. She closed her eyes for a moment. Obviously, they hadn't fully succeeded.

The witch had called her a pawn and had used her as such in whatever game she was playing. Now her father was dead—by her own hand. *The witch will pay for using me like this,* she thought. A chill seemed to wrap itself around her and the girl shivered.

"Do not presume to lift your hand to me!" She heard Malei's voice in her head. The witch had cast some sort of magic with those words. She knew she would not be able to do anything against her. Her hand tightened on the hilt of the blade and she concentrated on returning to Malei's office.

~ * ~

Malei paced her office; the mirror had gone blank after Pawn had completed her task and it was taking longer than it should have for the girl to be returned. A sudden chill filled the room as a mist began to form. She raised her staff and whispered the words of an emotion calming spell. Between that spell and the protections she had woven on that first day, she should be safe.

The mist shimmered as the girl stepped out. She dropped the bloodstained dagger on the table. "Next time, do your own dirty work, witch!"

Malei looked at Pawn and grinned. The girl's eyes were now a brilliant sapphire. The previous spells placed on her were broken. The Pawn was no more; there was only an angry young woman with a major decision to face.

Malei passed her hand over the knife and the blood vanished.

"What is this?" Pawn started to reach for the dagger, but stopped herself from actually touching it.

"It was only an illusion, a test. You killed no one tonight." Malei reached behind her to the shelf, picked up the dusty alicorn pendant, and laid it on the desk next to the knife. "In chess, when a pawn reaches the other side of the board it is promoted; sometimes to the most powerful piece on the board. Now that you know what it is to be a Pawn and subject to the whims of another you are ready to be a Queen," she said.

Pawn stared at her for a moment. "Then my father…"

"Is still alive."

"But you tried to take his throne before. Why do this? Why use me? If it was only an illusion, are you planning to enchant me again so I will kill him for you?"

Malei shook her head. "No, child. What I have done and what I do is to preserve and protect this kingdom."

The girl reached for the pendant, and Malei trapped her hand before she could remove it from the desk. "If you pick up that pendant, you will have no memory of this place or of me. You will be returned to your family, and it will seem as if you have awakened from a long sleep. You will no longer have a choice in what you do. You will be required to fulfill the role your family has laid out for you. However, you will perform that role exceptionally well because of your time here."

Malei removed her hand from Pawn's. "On the other hand, if you pick up the dagger, you will be permitted to remain here and continue your training. You have within you the potential to be a great leader. The choice is yours." She paused for a moment. "Before you choose, I have one other question. What was your opinion of the request brought before you during the session with Pyrin?"

"I agreed with the proposal."

"Why?"

"By ensuring everyone is able to read, they are less susceptible to rumor and superstition. It is easier for those who govern to make sure their message is delivered properly if it is written out instead of hoping nothing is misspoken if it is only heralded."

Malei nodded. "You are ready to choose." She waved her hand over the knife and the pendant. As her hand passed over the blade the blood reappeared.

"Know this; whether you decide to stay or leave, you will one day have to live with another's blood on your hands. Whether you spill that blood yourself or order it spilled, either way you are the one responsible. You should also understand your responsibilities to those you lead and serve must come before personal loyalties. There may come a time when you will have to sacrifice someone or something you care deeply about to protect those who look to you for protection.".

The girl hesitated as her hand wavered over the bloody dagger and the silver necklace. "Wasn't it you who taught me that sometimes we must put personal desires aside in the name of duty because it is in the best interest of those we would serve and have serve us?"

Malei nodded once. "I am proud of you, Aurora. You have learned your lessons well. Pick up the pendant and claim your birthright."

"Why did you do this to me?" Aurora demanded.

"Because I was once as you are now." Malei reached up and removed a slender silver chain from under her dress; on it hung a silver alicorn identical to Aurora's. "As the eldest, I believed I would be the better choice to rule. However, my father was adamant a woman could not rule and gave what should have been my birthright to my brother—your father. Since then, I have remained here, protecting the kingdom with my magic and keeping a watchful eye on the royal family. My mother was the only child of the previous king and when she married, her husband was crowned as the heir and she became subservient to him. Fortunately, they married while her parents were still ruling and he came to love this kingdom and the people here so that he was a good ruler. I worry that there will come a day when someone will marry into the royal line just to take control of our land and subjugate it to another. Because of who you are, there are many who will want to control you in order to control what is rightfully yours. I have given you the training to prevent this. You will no longer be a pawn. Not for me, not for your parents or anyone else."

Aurora picked up the pendant and fell to the floor. A spot of blood was on her finger where the horn of the alicorn had pricked her. Malei stepped around the desk and carefully placed the necklace around the girl's neck. She then spoke the words of an another spell and the sleeping girl vanished from the room.

Malei passed her hand over the mirror and watched as the girl appeared in the sleeping chamber of a high tower at the palace. She clutched the silver alicorn pendant at her neck as she watched the scene unfold in the polished surface. A young man was there, frozen in time as he leaned over the girl. The prince who had passed his own tests in reaching the castle to kiss Aurora.

A blue light glowed in the room and the man stirred slowly. He looked at the sleeping princess, then leaned over and gently kissed her.

Aurora's eyes fluttered as she woke. Her hand went to the silver pendant she wore before she reached up to kiss her prince.

~ * ~

As the spell completely faded, Malei watched the rest of the castle waking up from their long sleep. She spent not much time at it, however, for she had other pressing business to attend to. She did wonder, briefly, how the legends would be written about the sleeping princess who had waited one hundred years to be awakened by her prince, now that Aurora had no memory of her time with her aunt.

It was an amusing thought. She would probably be labeled as an evil witch!

Third Time's the Charm

"Well that was the last one." Brian put his computer tablet on the ledge and looked down at the body of the large bird.

"Saved from near extinction for a few centuries, the California Condor has finally followed in the steps of one of its distant ancestors."

Brian turned to see his partner, Walter standing next to him. "You've confirmed the genetic timeline?"

"Yep. The California Condor evolved from dinosaurs. One of the largest birds—unfortunately, we can't prove which dinosaur line evolved into which avian line. Although, I like to think of them as evolving from T-Rex. Seems fitting."

Brian shook his head. "T-Rex; some say he was the greatest predator that ever lived, not counting man. Selected for extinction as a dinosaur—managed to evolve into a bird which was again selected for extinction, then saved by intervention..."

"The Condor wasn't selected for extinction—it was man's interference that almost caused that one," Walter said interrupting Brian.

"Man is a part of nature—no matter what others say. Still, the Condor was on the brink of extinction and was saved. Now, it has finally lost the battle."

Walter nodded and looked down at the body of dead condor. "Well as they say—third time's the charm."

Midnight Ritual

Harailt reined his horse in and took a few minutes to study the village before him. His father ordered him here after finding out he had been studying magic. As a minor noble, perhaps because he was only a minor noble, his father had been quick to prevent the scandal that would have happened if anyone had learned one of his sons was consorting with *evil*. He pressed a hand against the papers he carried in his pocket and smiled as he continued to look at the village. Although his father's decision to send him here had been strictly a political ploy to protect their family's position, he, as well as the Lady Acacia had written him letters of introduction to a woman named Briana who was the healer for this small community.

He shook his head as his gaze rested on the building in the center of the village. Even here, where the power of the old ways was rumored to still be strong, a church of the Christ stood. He didn't understand the attitude of many these days. At one time, they welcomed the Fey and their magic, now they shunned and reviled them—all because some priest told them to do so. Surely, there was nothing evil in a tool, only in the way it was used. But, these priests wanted to argue that only their God and those who represented him should have that type of power. They said those who used magic to change the world around them, instead of using hard work and toil, were challenging God's authority and therefore could only have gained their power through some sort of pact with the demons who once rebelled against their God. Still, if this Briana was known as a woman of power, then perhaps the priests didn't have as strong a hold over these people as they did in other places.

Harailt tightened his knees slightly and his horse began working his way down the narrow path to the village.

~ * ~

"We will be performing the ritual at the Solstice," Briana said

161

as her gaze moved from Leathan to his younger brother, Stephan. She felt a chill wrap itself around her as she looked again at Leathan. His form wavered and she heard a mournful howl fill her ears as he dropped to the floor and shifted into a wolf. Another image overlaid Leathan's; Adairia, tears shimmered in her dark blue eyes and her black hair hung lank and dull. A shadow passed over Leathan but there was something else there, a feeling of hope and rebirth. She blinked and the images faded.

"You still plan to ask Adairia to marry you, despite the risks" she said.

"I still do not understand why I cannot stand alone during the ritual," Stephen said interrupting Leathan.

Briana shook her head. "That is not the way the binding works. All children of the current generation must partake in the ritual or we all will be cursed." She hid the sorrow she felt after her vision with a smile. "It is probable you will be the one chosen to serve as Guardian, Stephen. Yours is the willing heart with no ties to another. While I do not understand how the ritual chooses whom it does, it has never claimed one unwilling—when there was a willing heart."

"However, you still feel my proposal to Adairia is inappropriate." Leathan's gaze was locked with hers for a moment then he dropped it to the floor.

Briana felt him flinch as she reached out and took hold of his chin and forced him to look up at her. "If you love her, then you will wait until after the ritual to continue your relationship. Would you ask her to suffer losing you if you are the one chosen to serve?"

"No." He paused and took a deep breath. "May I tell her the reasons? She should be allowed to understand what the risks are and make her decision based on knowing. It is also not fair for her to be put off at this point and then if I am chosen to serve to never know what happened to me."

"She is an outsider," Stephen said.

Briana stepped back and nodded. "He is correct. However…," She raised her hand to stop Leathan's protest. "However, I do agree—she should know what might happen. The two of you are bound together—true soul mates—through life, death and unto life again." She closed her eyes and saw Leathan as the wolf with Adairia. "Yes." She nodded her head slowly. "She should know about the ritual. Let her make the decision once she knows the risks."

Leathan nodded. "Thank you."

"Be careful," Stephen said. "The nature of our family's guardianship has been a tightly held secret for several generations."

"I understand," he whispered.

"Leathan," Briana whispered. "She must know all of the risks—not just the risk you may be chosen, but also that one of your children may be called as Guardian in the future."

"Do we have your blessing?"

Briana nodded. "If you explain everything to her and she agrees, then you do indeed have my blessing. However, there will be no formal engagement or announcements until after the ritual is completed."

Leathan bowed his head then left.

Briana watched her grandsons leave her shop. *Bound together— true soul mates,* she thought. *Through life, death and unto life again.* She smiled. Yes, Leathan and Adairia would face sorrow, but they would come through it together.

~ * ~

Harailt reined in his horse and paused at the sight of a field of heather. Most of the heather in this area should have already begun to lose its flowers as summer was coming to an end, yet here was a field still in full bloom. He pushed back the hood of his cloak and nodded as a young woman waved at him from where she sat among the flowers. Her dark hair shimmered in the noon sun.

"Welcome to Cywynd," she called.

"Thank you," he said. He remained on his horse, not dismounting as he continued to watch her. "Can you direct me to the Healer Briana?"

"She runs the apothecary shop," the girl said. "It is located across the road from the church." She pointed toward the west. "The road you are on will take you by it. However, I do not believe she is there at this time."

"She will be returning to the shop in about two hours," a young man said as he approached the girl.

Harailt saw the girl smile at the other man and frowned. He was plain, dressed in the clothes of a tradesman. Not the fine clothes he, even as the last son born to a minor lord, wore. A woman this beautiful should be the wife of someone who could give her the things she deserved. He looked at the young man and moved his fingers slowly then muttered a phrase Lady Acacia had taught him. Before he could grasp the magic of the spell he felt something twist it away from the target. He snapped his fingers to release the power back to the elements, but wasn't sure he had done so properly.

"There is a small tavern located a short walk from the church, which also has rooms for rent," the young man said bowing slightly. "My Lord."

Harailt inclined his head slightly. "Thank you for the information." He kicked his horse and headed toward the town.

He glanced back at the couple standing amongst the lavender and white blooms and frowned. There were protective magics woven about the young man. And there was something else—he was a member of the clan the Guardians came from. The previous Guardian had been slain only a few weeks ago, the clan would have to choose a new one soon. There had to be a way to affect the ritual so the one chosen was the one he wanted to serve.

~ * ~

Briana ignored the young man standing before her, his back stiff, as she read the letters he had given her.

"Very interesting," she said when she finished and looked up. "Am I to believe a son of Lord Ryland wishes to pursue the paths of magic? Paths that will bring you pain and sorrow. Paths that could destroy your family's position."

"You have my father's letter," he said. His gaze locked with hers.

She frowned at the arrogance she saw in his brown eyes. "I want to hear it from you. If I am to train you, then you must understand your place."

"My place," he said as he straightened his shoulders. "My place has been dictated by my father who sent me here. *Your* place is to teach me."

"I do not believe so." She held the papers back out to him.

"Unless you can explain why you wish to follow this path; I cannot help you."

"Lady Acacia once told me it is the power that chooses whom it wills. I have the power; therefore, I have little choice in following this path."

"She probably also told you that one who held power, yet was untrained was very dangerous. There are ways to block your power so you need not follow this path. I believe she would have told you that also."

"She did." He still held his head high not taking his gaze from hers.

She focused her Sight on him and felt him shudder as he was unable to look away from her. There was a great deal of power there as well as a dark shadow surrounding him, one that would bring pain to many others. This she did not like. Still he was correct, the power chose whom it willed and there were so few being born with the gift she couldn't just block his power until she knew the path he would tread—but by then she might not be able to.

When she finally released his gaze, she saw his hands trembling. *Good,* she thought. *He now understands something of my power.*

"You do have access to power, Harailt, but there is no indication of which path you are to walk. This I do not like."

"Which path?"

"Your path is what would show me the skills you should be trained in. There are those who walk the path of service—they are the ones who seek to help others and seem to bring hope and joy with them. There are those who walk the path of self—they are the ones who seek power only for themselves. They wish to control the world around them, wanting only what benefits them. Finally, there are those who walk the narrow path between the two. They seek power for its own sake, yet will not turn away from those whom they can help and do not deliberately seek to injure or hurt others."

She focused her Sight again and waited for him to answer. The dark shadow wavered and she saw a thin band of grey between it and Harailt. "Which path would you wish to follow?" She held up a hand to stop his response. "Do not answer hastily, or with the answer you think I would want to hear. If you walk the wrong path from ignorance you risk almost as much as if you had chosen in order to deceive."

"I would walk the third path," he said.

The grey band grew and she smiled. "Very well. I will train you," she said. "But be warned; if you stray from this path again, your power will be bound; by your own doing."

She watched his eyes grow wider then motioned to the back room.

~ * ~

Harailt glanced up from the herbs he was sorting and nodded to the young woman who had entered the small apothecary shop. It was the same woman he had spoken to when he first arrived here in this town. "Good day to you," he said. He had to force himself to blink as he found himself staring into her dark blue eyes. Eyes that were so dark they almost appeared black. Her long black hair hung over her shoulders like a cloak. For the first time he was glad his father had exiled him to this remote place. And, for just an instant he even forgot the reasons he had been sent away.

"And to you," she said offering him a soft smile. "I am in need of the following items." She handed him a piece of paper. "My mother has developed a severe cough that has lasted for several days."

He hesitated before taking the paper and glancing at it. The handwriting was neat and delicate, but there was strength in the way the letters were written. Very much, he suspected, like the lady herself. She had left nothing off her list that would normally be recommended for the treatment of a lingering cough and that was also telling. She had knowledge of herb lore and medicines.

"We have everything you have listed available. I will be only a few moments." He looked up from the paper, nodded, then moved to the back room.

As he gathered the requested items, he frowned. He had felt a pricking along his spine when she told him about her mother. He had targeted his spell at the young man who approached that day, but it had been prevented from striking him by protective magics. He thought he had dispersed the power properly but it now appeared it had instead found another target. With care he whispered a few words of power over the herbs. It was his fault Adairia's mother was ill; therefore, he should attempt to restore the Balance and aid in her recovery.

"You have not expended your power for any others who have come here seeking remedies for their ailments, why this time?" Briana asked.

"Remember your admonishment about not straying from the path again."

She nodded.

"I believe that because of that, I am the one responsible for the woman's ailment. My aid in this matter will help to restore the balance I destroyed," he said.

"As long as that is the only reason." Briana frowned then turned and left the room.

He stood there for a moment staring at the doorway. The woman was too perceptive sometimes. He quickly prepared the herbs and carried them out to Adairia.

"I hope your mother feels better soon," he said handing her the packet.

"Thank you." She laid a coin on the counter.

"Adairia. Tomorrow will be the night of the Solstice. I would like to ask you to attend the festival with me." The words came out in a rush.

Adairia smiled. "I'm sorry, but I will be attending with Leathan. We hope to announce our engagement tomorrow."

"Tomorrow? Wouldn't tonight be a better occasion?"

"Normally, yes. But, we must wait until after Briana completes the Guardian Ritual tonight."

"My apologies. I had forgotten about that. May the ritual conclude in your favor," he said.

"Thank you."

He watched as Adairia left the shop. The ritual to determine the new Guardian would be tonight. Briana had refused to give him this information when he had asked about it. She had said only those members of the clan who might be affected by the ritual and herself would be allowed to be present. Despite the oaths to his family that bound her clan to their guardianship of this land, he was still not permitted to be there.

Briana must be concerned Leathan might be chosen as Guardian if Adairia knew enough of what was going on to be aware of the ritual and when it would be held. He would make sure he was there as well.

~ * ~

Briana watched as Leathan and Adairia danced together during the last dance of the festival. While they had told no one of their engagement, the two had taken the opportunity presented to enjoy each other's company as if this had been their wedding celebration. She hoped this would not be the only celebration they were able to enjoy.

She nodded as they joined her, followed by Stephen. A quick glance up at the moon showed it was almost time for the ritual to begin. She could sense Harailt nearby and frowned. His power had grown considerably in the time he had been with her and she doubted she would be able to bind it properly, but now that his path had finally defined itself, she knew she would have to try. What was concerning her at this time was that he might try to interfere in the ritual. She had seen his interest in Adairia and while he might try to convince her and himself the reason he had enhanced the healing powers of the herbs was to restore the balance he had disrupted; she knew it was because he cared about Adairia.

His family was the one who had laid the binding on her clan that required them to serve as guardians. He had asked her several times about the ritual and when the new guardian would be chosen. Now, she was worried he might know a way to influence the choice that would be made tonight.

She moved her fingers through a complicated pattern and whispered a quick warding charm as she walked with her grandsons toward the clearing.

~ * ~

Harailt watched from the shadows of the trees as Briana walked around the stone circle. Adairia waited outside the circle and he could see the worry she felt as she twisted her hands together. He forced his attention away from Adairia and back to Briana and the two men. The woman was still walking around the stone ring and a mist was slowly rising from the ground. He caught his breath as the howl of a wolf came from nearby followed by several more.

He finally released his breath as several large black wolves walked past him and into the ring. He blinked as the wolves shimmered in the moonlight and realized these were not common wolves; these were spectral creatures—probably the spirits of the previous guardians.

Briana now stood in the center of the circle and Leathan and Stephen stood one in front and the other behind her as the wolves walked the path Briana had previously followed.

"Ages past, our clan bound itself to this land, as guardians of all who dwell here and the magic that binds all life together," Briana said. "The one who was guardian has passed beyond the veil and it is now time for a new guardian to be chosen."

Harailt smiled as several of the wolves stopped in front of Leathan and touched their noses to his hand. Now was the time. He began chanting softly, hoping to influence the rest of the pack in making their choice.

"No!"

The whispered exclamation broke his concentration and he turned to see Adairia staring at him in the darkness. He took a step back, deeper into the shadows and hoped she hadn't recognized him. Unfortunately, it was now too late for him to influence the choice made by the wolves. The largest of the spectral wolves walked over to Stephen and took his hand in his mouth.

Harailt frowned as the mist in the clearing flowed toward and surrounded Stephen. All of the wolves raised their heads and howled. When the mist dissipated, a large wolf stood where Stephen had been.

"The choice has been made," Briana said.

Harailt shuddered as Briana's gaze moved from the wolf to where he was standing among the trees. There was a flash of light in her eyes and he found himself surrounded by the spectral wolves. "You will remain here until the others have left. Then we will talk," he heard Briana whisper.

"Stephen, you have been chosen as the Guardian for this land. To you falls the task of watching over all those who dwell here. You are charged with protecting the Balance," Briana said.

The wolf bowed his head.

"Go. Run with the pack for this moon. Live as they do. Learn from them. Return to us ready to serve."

The wolf turned and vanished into the forest.

"Leathan and Adairia." She held out her hands. "You have my blessings on your marriage." She paused. "However, understand there are no others who can take up the mantle of Guardian if something should happen to Stephen. I wish you both only happiness, but know the path you would walk together, may eventually hold sorrow. Take pleasure in each other and find happiness in all things."

"We will," Leathan said taking Adairia's hand.

"I will speak to the priest tomorrow. The announcement will be posted and the ceremony will take place at the next full moon."

Another month, Harailt thought. He had another month before they would be married and Briana had just told him how to prevent it.

~ * ~

Briana waited as Leathan and Adairia returned to Cywynd; she had other business to attend to this night. "Harailt," she whispered. "Step into the circle."

She frowned as the young man stepped out of the trees and the spectral wolves herding him faded into the night. She hadn't dismissed them yet. Had he managed to do so without her sensing it? This was not a good sign.

"You have strayed from the path you told me you wanted to follow," she said. "I see now your path will be one of pain—pain brought to others. This I cannot allow."

"You cannot allow." Harailt snorted as he glared at her. "I do not believe you have any control over what I do or do not do at this point."

"Fear and hatred of those like us continues to grow. To allow one such as yourself to walk the path now will only cause more harm to others. I have a duty to prevent that. Just as my clan is bound to its guardianship of this land, I am bound to my own guardianship." She raised her hands as tendrils of mist rose around her and Harailt. She knew she couldn't bind his power completely, but she could control it and limit the harm he was able to do.

"You have chosen your path, but your power is bound until such time you find another to walk the path with you."

"Briana, I want none other than Adairia and I will only accept her. I will relinquish all my power to you if you are able to prevent me from separating her and Leathan. Otherwise, know they will be separated forever."

"You have set the final terms and are bound by them."

"Agreed. I offer one other wager. I will separate them before the end of the next full moon."

Briana frowned. "And if you succeed?"

"I get the book you hold—the Weaver's book."

Briana paused. He wanted the Weaver's book, but couldn't fully understand its power. He would still be able to use his power if he had the book, but who would be controlling that power. Harailt was strong, but not strong enough to prevent the book from controlling him. She also knew he had heard her warning to Leathan and Adairia and would go after Stephen as a way to force Leathan into the guardianship. Stephen was now vulnerable. If Harailt succeeded, and there was a chance he would do so, he would get the book. She would have to find a way to limit the damage the book would cause in his hands.

"Agreed." She held out her hand.

~ * ~

Harailt clutched the black book tightly to protect it from the wind suddenly swirling around him. How long had it been since the last time he visited this place? It seemed forever. The village of Cywynd was no more—only a few crumbling buildings and this small graveyard remained. He smiled when he saw the spell he had placed on this grave was still functioning and a wreath of heather appeared in front of the marker just as the first rays of the morning sun touched the gray stone. "Adairia," he whispered her name.

"She is no longer here." Harailt heard a familiar voice say.

"Impossible." He turned to find himself staring into gray eyes that were unblinking. "I know the curse you laid on me keeps me bound to this plane, but how is it you are still here?"

"Because the final outcome of that binding has yet to be decided. An outcome that will be determined tonight."

"No!" He took a step back from Briana. "The outcome was decided long ago. You gave me the book as was agreed and I have not relinquished my power."

Briana smiled and shook her head. "That is true, but your power has been bound none-the-less. It is only because you possess the Weaver's Book you can wield the limited power you do. The final condition of the binding was that you would separate Leathan and Adairia forever. Tonight will test whether that is true or not."

"How can that be, she died long ago and Leathan, though bound by his guardianship, surely has passed as well."

"Again you have underestimated what you do not understand." Briana held out her hand. "Come with me and we will see how this night ends—together."

Harailt nodded once then took her hand. A mist rose from the ground and surrounded them, obscuring his sight. When it cleared, he was standing next to Briana in the shadows of a large tree. In front of them was a small church and graveyard; three people sat talking near one of the graves.

"Do you still trust my powers?" Briana whispered.

"I never doubted your power," he said.

"Then trust me now." Briana raised her hands and the mist again surrounded them creating cloaks that would hide them from the others. She nodded toward the graveyard.

Harailt moved closer to the trio. "Adairia?" he spoke the name before he could stop himself.

The woman looked up and he could see the glow of the moon shimmering around and through her. *A ghost. She has been trapped here all this time as a ghost and I never sensed this.* Adairia turned back to the other two men. "Forgive me, Father, for I have sinned," she said.

"It was this sin which condemned you to remain here?" One of the men said.

Harialt studied the man for a moment. He was no longer young, nor was he aged. His face held lines of experience and his eyes spoke of wisdom and compassion. He appeared to be one of the rare followers of the Christ who accepted there were faiths other than his own and did not judge others simply because of their faith.

"Yes," he heard Adairia say. "It condemned Leathan, also."

Leathan? How is this possible? He should have been trapped as the guardian; yet here he is—human. He moved closer to Leathan and raised his hand. A tendril of mist wove itself around Leathan. A picture formed before him, a picture of the night his curse had struck Leathan, the night these two had been married.

The wedding and celebration had continued until late and it had been close to midnight before Leathan and Adairia had left to go to the house they were to share. The lantern Leathan carried illuminated the sprays of heather woven around the door as they approached.

"Leathan, they're beautiful," Adairia said, taking one the sprays and holding it close to her face.

"Lady Adairia, if I may?" Leathan held his arms out to her.

"Of course." She wrapped her arms around him and kissed him lightly as he started to gather her in his arms.

Harailt cringed as he felt the sudden burning that coursed down Leathan's limbs and began to engulf his whole body.

"No!" Adairia cried.

Just as suddenly as it started, the pain stopped. Harailt smiled as he watched Adairia back away from the now changed Leathan, the spray of heather she had been holding now dropped. "No. No. No." She turned and fled. A plaintive howl following her.

He remembered Adairia going to Briana; her sobs as she tried to tell Leathan's grandmother about what had happened.

Briana had guided Adairia into her shop and that was the last he had seen of her. It had been only a few months later she had died. Even then Briana would not acknowledge he had fulfilled the final requirement of the binding; insisting, as she had earlier, it was his own words that Leathan and Adairia would be separated forever. Now, he understood why. Something had bound these two together—trapping them on the mortal plane unable to pass beyond the veil. He looked at Briana and saw the sadness in her eyes. "You knew."

"I didn't know the specifics. But, I knew they were bound together through life, unto death and even unto life again," she said. "If I had known they would be trapped like this, I would have found a way to prevent it—even if the price was to unleash your power."

"It was their love that bound them in this way. A love I tried to come between. I was wrong." He held the book out to Briana.

She raised her hand to refuse the book, then nodded toward

Leathan and Adairia; Harialt turned.

"Adairia, be free," Leathan whispered lifting her hands to his lips. He released her hands, stood and stepped back slowly.

The priest raised his cross and the moonlight grew stronger and bathed Adairia as she began to fade from view.

"No!" she cried. "Leathan, I do not want to leave you."

"She would choose to remain trapped like this? To stay with him?" Harailt asked.

"She would. And he would choose to release her knowing he would remain trapped; if she would be freed from this."

Harailt dropped his head. He realized just how shallow his love had been. In the name of love, he had stripped Adairia from the person she loved more than life—then because of her grief, she had let herself die and be trapped in this pitiful existence. Neither dead nor alive and still separated from Leathan. Leathan loved her enough to let her go. While his possessiveness had destroyed her. Briana was right; he could not be trusted to use his power properly.

The moonlight faded and the mist swirled, concealing Adairia from sight. When the fog lifted, a female wolf stood where Adairia had been.

Harailt watched as Leathan changed from a human to a wolf. While he felt a slight tingling in his limbs, he was not assaulted by pain as he had been when he had been in Leathan's memories of that first night. He smiled when he saw Leathan now standing nose to nose with Adairia.

"Go in peace, my children." The priest made the sign of the cross over the two wolves. "My blessings and God's on you both. May you always find sanctuary and welcome in this place."

"You were correct," Harailt said after the two wolves disappeared into the trees and the priest had returned to the building.

"However, I was not correct about you." She nodded toward the book he still held and he handed it to her.

"You are not ready to hold this book. It will continue to influence you, but in a few years I believe you will be a worthy successor to its guardianship."

Harailt stared at the hand she held out to him. "You are willing to take me back as a student."

"I am. I have seen your true heart this night. There is still a chance for you to return to the path; if you are willing."

He grasped her hand, glanced toward the trees the wolves had vanished into and smiled. "I have learned much over the centuries I have been trapped by my own foolishness. Tonight, I learned that I still have much to learn and much to atone for. I am willing."

"Good. Then come with me beyond the first veil into the realm where magic still exists and I will teach you." Mist surrounded them and Harailt felt warmth as the area around them faded from sight.

About the Author

A native Texan, Carol found her way to her current home in Colorado by way of a five-year detour in The Nederlands - courtesy of her husband Tim and the US Air Force.

An avid reader at a young age, her strong desire to write came from her love of (her husband calls it her obsession with) Star Trek. It was this early love of Star Trek that led her to the Science Fiction and Fantasy genres.

In addition to her writing she has worked as a receptionist/office manager for two veterinary clinics, a deputy sheriff in El Paso County Colorado and for the Professional Bull Riders.

She has been published in various anthologies and magazines including "Creature Fantastic", PanGaia Magazine, "Stories of Strength", Baen's Universe, Tales of the Talisman and Kepler's Dozen. Her books include: *Call of Chaos*, *Chaos Embraced*, *The Road into Chaos*, and *Chaos Challenged*.

Carol has also edited several anthologies for Sky Warrior Books including: "Zombiefied", "These Vampires Don't Sparkle", and "The Dragon's Hoard".

In addition to her own writing, she is the editor and publisher of the online e-zine: The Lorelei Signal as well as running her own micro-press – WolfSinger Publications.

You can visit her online at www.carolhightshoe.com

Other Books by Carol Hightshoe

Call of Chaos - Book One: The Chaos Reigns Saga

The exiled daughter of a minor noble, Kyrianna Dalynne, finds herself trapped in a temple dedicated to Thynitic, The Lady of Chaos. She and her companions, are charged with finding an ancient artifact before the ones guarding the portals out will allow them to leave. As their search continues, Kyrianna begins to question if there was a specific reason she and the others were brought to this place.

After the guardians claim the artifact has been secured, they offer to open the portals to allow the group to return to their homes. Instead of the familiar forest of Kilenter, Kyrianna finds herself in another world. Her companions from the temple arrive several days after her.

When one of the members is accused of murder, they are tasked with assisting Tristan Duvall, who must face the demons and ghosts of his family's past in order to claim his birthright as a nobleman of the city of Raspa. Kyrianna finds herself attracted to the young man and facing the difficult decision of accepting his invitation to remain with him or return to her own home.

Chaos Embraced – Book Two: The Chaos Reigns Saga

Nowhere in all the worlds or planes is there no pain, torment or chaos. All we can do is accept those strikes which cannot be avoided and give back chaos and pain to those who offend. Kindness should be the only companion to pain and will increase the intensity of suffering and the chaos surrounding us. Do not ignore the sudden whim of compassion; let it always come, but only seldom as to give those who suffer a sense of hope. Hope is consort to chaos and torment is their offspring. Unending torment destroys pain and this in turn destroys the chaos that nurtures us. Act alluring to trap those who would never seek the Lady on their own. Confuse those that think they know the ways of the world around them. Bring pain and torment not only to those who enjoy it,

or to those who deserve it, but also to the innocent and those who do not antic-
ipate it. The lash, fire and cold are the three physical pains that never fail the
devout. Love, jealousy and hatred are the three pains that should follow in the
footsteps of her devout. Spread Thynitic's theology whenever pain is meted out
and chaos swirls. Wherever pain is, there is Thynitic. Wherever chaos is, there
is Thynitic. Embrace the pain and chaos. Embrace Thynitic.

Trapped in a place where they are constantly faced with new opponents and challenges, Kyrianna and her friends, will also have to face the Goddess Thynitic and her Chosen Torliana.

Kyrianna finds Thynitic whispering in her mind, calling her deeper into the chaos. In order to save her friends from the evil goddess, will she finally Embrace the Chaos and accept her place as a Daughter of Chaos or will she succeed in renouncing Thynitic forever? And if she does, what will the cost be?

The Road Into Chaos - Book Three: The Chaos Reigns Saga

After escaping from Thynitic's control, Kyrianna and her friends find themselves back on Shokar. All but one—Brular, the priest of Hellavar, who sacrificed his freedom to protect them, is now a prisoner of the Lady of Chaos.

Each member of the group is given a different vision to follow as they seek aid in rescuing Brular in the short time they have before they must journey into the Abyss to challenge Thynitic herself.

As they seek aid from various areas of Shokar, they find their efforts blocked by the temples of Mykaylene and Hellavar. They also learn others are preparing for a coming war against a group they only call the Faithless.

All of them find something unexpected, including Kyrianna—who finds a way to return home as well as an unexpected romantic entanglement.

Kyrianna must make choices—to accept her feelings for Tristan Duvall and risk losing her friend and companion—the unicorn Cewyr. To return home, to a family willing to welcome her back or face the Goddess Thynitic and eventually her own destiny as a Daughter of Chaos.

FOR A FRIEND

Those were Hendandra's words when the group was asked to go to the Abyss to rescue Brular from Thynitic.

Now they find themselves facing the horrors of that cursed place, along with nightmares from their own past as they struggle to reach the Lady of Chaos' citadel.

The closer they get to their goal the more dangerous their journey becomes and another deity enters the game—one who says she opposes Thynitic, but whose actions indicate she also wants to stop Kyrianna and her friends from facing the Lady of Chaos.

Even as she tries to fight her destiny as a Daughter of Chaos, Kyrianna finds herself being drawn deeper into Thynitic's plans.

Will she finally be able to separate herself from her destiny when she faces Thynitic or will the Lady of Chaos finally be able to claim her soul?